BISON
BOOKS

A TICKET

FOR A

SEAMSTITCH

HENRY W. WIGGEN

but polished for the printer by

MARK HARRIS

University of Nebraska Press
Lincoln and London

First Bison Book printing: April 1984
Most recent printing indicated by the first digit below:
2   3   4   5   6   7   8   9   10

Library of Congress Cataloging in Publication Data
Harris, Mark, 1922–
    A ticket for a seamstitch.
    I. Title.
PS3515.A757T5   1985   813'.54   84-25627
ISBN 0-8032-7224-3 (pbk.)

"Easy Does It Not" was first published in *The Living Novel,* ed.
Granville Hicks, Macmillan, 1957.

The quotation on page 85 is from THE TUMULT AND THE SHOUTING *by
Grantland Rice. Copyright 1954 by A. S. Barnes & Company, Inc.
Reprinted by permission of A. S. Barnes & Company, Inc.*

*The Special Souvenir Scorecard, provided for the convenience of readers, is
reprinted by courtesy of The New York Mammoths Baseball Club, Inc.*

for **RALPH GRAVES**

Preface: Easy Does It Not

> After you have made a diagnosis of the mechanical faults that may be causing you to read slowly, you are ready to apply remedial measures. . . . For all practice you should be sure to use EXTREMELY EASY AND RELATIVELY WORTHLESS READING MATERIAL, usually stories.
> —*Reading Rapidly and Well*, Wrenn and Cole

LET ME BEGIN in close.

I happen to own a left-handed baseball pitcher named Henry Wiggen. His teammates on the New York Mammoths call him "Author." I own the Mammoths, too. Indeed, I own the whole damn league, all the cities and all the players and all their wives and children. It is great fun. In collaboration, Henry and I have written three novels about our league.

Henry's left arm is his fortune, but his ear is his soul. He listens not to what people say but to what they mean. His report upon what he hears is frank, but he is armed against reprisal: his enemies, since they are invariably malicious (which is to say, stupid), have not the ears to know they have been condemned. If the reader is himself without ears (which is to say, untrained to read) he will think Henry untrained to write. He will think, Henry is nothing but a baseball player.

Among Henry's admirers are several gentlemen with the rank of Associate Editor or better at *Life* magazine. One day, on behalf of these gentlemen, a letter was sent to me asking whether, by chance, I had available a Henry Wiggen story which I might send to them for possible publication in the issue for July 2, 1956. I replied No, I had none at the moment. But I had an *idea,* I said. I outlined my idea, and they were delighted. They formalized matters with my agent, and *she* was delighted. Soon afterward I received an advance payment of $1,000. (Total payment for the story, upon acceptance, was to be at the rate of fifty cents a word, a sum likely to approach $10,000, or almost twice my annual salary as Instructor in English at San Francisco State College.) This $1,000 was mine to keep regardless of whether *Life* published the story: I was required only to deliver a manuscript.

I did not spend it. I put it in a safe place. Had I spent it I would have been committed to the completion of a project which, in the course of writing, I may have discovered was best left uncompleted. I thus reserved for myself the right of abandonment, for if my story should fail I could return to *Life* its $1,000 and keep to myself the unsuccessful manuscript.

The invitation could not have come at a more propitious time. We were in the midst of a busy semester at school, while about the house an extraordinary social season was in progress. These are, for me, the proper conditions for work, when morning and evening are crowded with talk and press, when I can make of my day a sandwich of four silent afternoon hours. For some weeks I lived a triangle, traveling from home to school, from school to a rented apartment where I worked on the *Life* story, thence home again.

The rented apartment was situated on the third floor of a dwelling on San Francisco's Downey Street. Below, children played in the St. Agnes schoolyard. Their cry was with me, and it was appropriate to my purpose, for I was writing a story whose climax occurs at a baseball game, July 4, 1956, in Moors Stadium (I own it) in New York City, in the presence of the cry of many people. The cry from below was a persistent guide toward the finale I was pursuing. It prevented me from straying.

Yet when I wandered to the window, as from time to time I did, I saw how this was no crowd at all, how it was, rather, children one by one, separate and special, even as my own children are, to me at least, separate and special. I write, I think, of persons, not of crowds. Thus, as I wrote, my ear knew the voice of my subject, and my eye knew its image.

I saw from the window a society whole and complete, insistent upon its laws and traditions, yet not unwilling, now and then, to experiment, a society of followers and leaders, and, occasionally, of rebels and heretics, a body of men and women between the ages of six and twelve possessing within it the genius both to conserve and to progress, to govern, regulate, restrict, limit, resist, yet also to improvise and advance. You will find many such playgrounds in the City of San Francisco, here at the Western edge of the Western World. "This habit," De Tocqueville found, "may be traced even in the schools, where the children in their games are wont to submit to rules which they have themselves established, and to punish misdemeanors which they have themselves defined."

Please do not mistake me. I do not believe we have achieved, in the United States of America, a community of perfect order. I do not share *Life's* confidence that we are "the most successful society in human history." But although in politics I usually oppose the incumbency, recoil from prevailing tastes, and find myself unable to affiliate in spirit or even in fact with any power bloc larger than the company of a few friends, my sense of comfort—of belonging to the nation—is more than illusion. I do not think I am of those writers who, *Life* says, "feel surrounded by sinister, hostile forces, even a Philistine conspiracy to control their thoughts. . . ." My books have regularly been published by capitalists and read by Philistines, and one of them has even been beamed to the nation on television at considerable expense by the United States Steel Corporation.

Everything, it seemed, was right, my days arranged, money in escrow. At last, after fifteen years at hard labor, I was to become national! In July my characters, my vision, I myself, would become known to 5,714,000 readers. I who had always felt myself to be living not quite without, and yet not quite within, the mainstream of the national life, was at last acceptable.

My plot was this:

A young lady writes to Henry Wiggen from "somewhere out West" to tell him that she will be in New York to watch the Mammoths play on July 4th. Henry is her hero. But Henry has a wife, and for this reason (he says) he attempts to transfer the young lady's affection from himself to Thurston Woods, inevitably called "Piney," a twenty-year-old catcher with a passion for women of the Hollywood type, fast motorcycles, and low-slung automobiles.

We follow the young lady's cross-country journey, wherein she is endangered but never quite violated (she says). She is delayed for a time at The Geographical Center of the United States Motel, whose owner's intentions toward her are ambiguous but who finally delivers her safely to New York. He has sworn upon a stack of Bibles that he will do so, and so (of course) he does.

Piney Woods discovers, when the girl arrives, that she is no beauty. His dream has overshot reality. He begins to discover, however, that love and charm may reside even within a form less divine than Hollywood specifies. He learns, too, that mechanical progress may ring hollow.

I wrote my story in four-hour stints, cooled it, retyped it, and mailed to to Ralph Graves, the Associate Editor with whom I was working. I was less than wholly satisfied, and as I awaited Mr. Grave's reaction my doubt mounted. It became apparent to me that, as I had written the story, I had been fearful of the manner in which I was dealing with certain subjects. Should I, perhaps, have avoided motorcycles and Bibles? Is not a man on a motorcycle, reading a Bible, the very image of the ideal citizen in the most successful society in human history? My fears had cramped my style. Would not a little prudence have been wise? Think how many imprudent things I might afterward do and say with $10,000 in my pocket!

Mr. Graves was delighted with the story. But he was returning it for revision. He sent a six-page letter with recommendations so technically admirable as to be irresistible. He sent, also, another $1,000. I have worked with fine editors over the years, and I have come to depend upon them—with Walter Pistole at Reynal & Hitchcock, with Louis Simpson, John Maloney, and Hiram Haydn at Bobbs-Merrill, with Al Hart at Macmillan, and with Joe Fox and Harold Strauss at Knopf. To this class, I now say, Ralph Graves belongs, and to him my story is dedicated: that which had been a good-enough story was fashioned, because he scolded, into something much more. Forget wordage, he said; do a novel if you can't do a story. Rest your fears, uncramp, shake loose, let fly, go fuller, go deeper, and this I did, and my story was soon a story no more but a novel (at the very least a $15,000 novel, computed at *Life* rates). Its plot was the plot I have described, Bibles and motorcycles and all, but it now had space to move and turn and wheel and sound and echo in. I felt it leaping and racing, joyous in its release from confinement, and I worked, now, not four hours a day but fourteen, long after the schoolyard was dark and the children home asleep, and when it was done I knew that I had done something I shall never quite do again, and my friends at *Life* knew what I had done, and they sent it up—up to the man upstairs—and he said No.

In a twinkling was a small fortune lost. Had I ever really counted upon it in the first place, and begun to live the life of a man worth fifty cents a word, I would have been in serious difficulty with myself and with my art. Fortunately, the $13,000 I did not have was essential neither to the pride nor to the happiness of my family, and we largely shared the sentiment of our friend the novelist Donald Wetzel, who wrote to me: "Anyhow I know you got paid something for it. I think, well good, just like when I tried to get a job there and didn't, bad as I needed one. I mean I still thought, well good."

I composed a dedication page, inserted it in the manuscript, and asked my agent to deliver the whole to my publisher, Alfred A. Knopf, Inc. Harold Strauss, my editor at Knopf, found it, he wrote (my immodesty appalls me, but this is relevant, I think), "a minor American masterpiece. Not to publish it . . . would be a disservice to American literature." He then sent it to *his* man upstairs—to Mr. Knopf—from whom I soon received a most flattering note: "I have read *A Ticket for a Seamstitch* with delight. It is a true work of art and I think absolutely flawless within the limits you have set for yourself."

Life published, in its issue for July 2, 1956, instead of my story, an excerpt ("one of the best episodes") from a novel by William Brinkley, an Assistant Editor on its staff. "Good-humored and broadly satirical," the novel was shortly to be distributed by the Book-of-the-Month Club, a factor which I assume left a strong impression upon the man upstairs, for the excerpt was preceded by a detailed account of the book's adventure in high finance: M-G-M had bought it for $400,000 ("a sliding scale on movie profits"), Denmark, England, and Holland had bought it; it "promises to be financially one of the most successful books of 1956. . . . Brinkley is expected to make a total of $600,000." The novel subsequently ascended, in four weeks, to the top of the *New York Times* best-seller list, where it spent the summer.

I saw, everywhere, its advertisement: "It's got the whole country laughing!"

I read what I could, and I barely smiled, and as I sought among my friends confirmation of my own judgment I came to realize that they had not read it and did not plan to, that "the whole country" was somebody somewhere else. A few of my friends had turned its pages in bookstores, as one will, had read *in* it, not laughed, closed it, and forgotten it. Yet we are not remote from life. We laugh, we have our passions.

In time, Mr. Brinkley disappeared, and the advertisement ceased. "I want to do fiction," says Mr. Brinkley, "learn how to write fiction." It is an engaging modesty, all the more affecting because his faith is the faith of innocence: if, at thirty-eight, Mr. Brinkley can really write no better than he writes now, he will never learn. He is certain that writing is easy, that there is nothing to it, that you put words together and form a vague picture of an action, and there you have it—lo!—writing. He did it easily, and it was easily read. When, in the autumn, I returned to school I discovered that my entering freshmen had read Mr. Brinkley, and that they had liked him. "Easy reading," they said.

My experience became meaningful to me, now, in a way it had not been. The passage of my manuscript through the uppermost offices of *Life* provided me with authority for this account. Who could have asked more for $13,000? I see at last a chief difficulty of American fiction: I see that a magazine like *Life* objects less to controversial subject matter than to difficult style. *Not irreverence, but craftsmanship, dismays the editors of mass media.*

There is easy reading. And there is literature. There are easy writers, and there are writers. There are people whose ears have never grown, or have fallen off, or have merely lost the power to listen. And there are people with ears.

II

I see, in GROSSINGER NEWS-NOTES, which I studiously read every Sunday on the Resorts page of the *New York Times,* the following: "Long distance honors of the week go to . . . Leon Carat and his sister, Lena, who are here from Paris, France." And only this moment my eye catches, in the same advertisement, word to the effect that "Herman WOUK, brilliant author," was at Grossinger's during the week Leon and Lena were there.

Or I call to mind that triumphant joke about the hopeful *Reader's Digest* contributor—he who had sexual intercourse with a bear in an iron lung for the FBI and found God.

Do you laugh? I laugh. My friends laugh. If you have ears you have a sense of the world, you know where Paris is, you have never gone to Grossinger's, you are not astonished to learn that Mr. Wouk vacations there, you do not read the

Digest. I once heard Groucho Marx, on the radio, attempt to convey the *Digest* joke. His studio audience responded with a profound silence. (Probably you have never been a member of a studio audience.) Yet the joke has traveled round and round and round the country, and raised, I am sure, a million voices in laughter. It delights men and women whose ears have caught the rhythm of the *Digest,* but who do not subscribe.

The life of our literature depends, like the life of a superb joke, upon private transmission, not upon television, radio, or magazines. The novelist depends upon that relatively small audience which brings to reading a frame of reference, a sophistication, a level of understanding not lower than the novelist's own. He cannot hope to touch the reader who comes in innocence, who must be told upon each occasion where Paris is, who demands, in short, that the novelist be easy, that he not require the reader to exert any part of himself but his eyeballs.

Such a reader is hopeless. "You must depend upon the reader to stretch his mind," Elizabeth Janeway once warned me. "You cannot stretch it for him." This I believe, and I resist, as *true* novelists do, the injunction (usually a worried editor's) to be clearer, to be easier, to explain, if I feel that the request is for the convenience of the reader at the expense of craft. The novelist jealous of his craft cannot write the Brinkley line:

"'Gentlemen,' he said humorously, switching on his electric-light smile . . ."

Rather, he writes for the reader who will decide for himself whether the speaker speaks with humor, and what kind of smile the speaker smiles. Or, if the novelist describes a smile, he will choose to do so with precision. He cannot reduce himself, cannot believe he is saying anything when he tells you, as Mr. Brinkley does, that someone sits "silent . . . as an owl," that someone "had the aspect of a man who tangled with one of the Seabee's bulldozers," or that people "looked like the survivors of a fierce naval engagement."

This is to say nothing, nothing at all, to hurry words onto paper as if they do not matter.

The novelist will set you down among his people, and he will leave you to inhabit their world with them, and you will perceive for yourself the habits and assumptions which shape motives. Shakespeare supplies no stage directions beyond bare information to the effect that people enter and exit, assigning to our imagination the task of forming from the speech of his people our notions of their character.

Robert Coughlan, a Staff Writer for *Life,* complains in *The Private World of William Faulkner,* that in *A Fable* "nothing is revealed directly if it can be done by reflection; episodes and conversations begin without prior references to known events or thoughts; nothing is said clearly if it can be obfuscated; characters appear from nowhere and disappear to nowhere; motivation and character development are inexplicable. The book, on the whole, seems demented." Even so, Mr. Coughlan "somehow" was "deeply and personally if irrationally involved in a great and infinitely tragic event."

What is wanted? That something infinitely tragic has been achieved is commendable, apparently, but the book is demented because Mr. Faulkner did not produce infinite tragedy straightforwardly, chronologically, systematically —did not make of his work "easy reading."

The charge against Mr. Faulkner is that he is difficult, and that he is afflicted by a "cosmic pessimism," a phrase which Mr. Coughlan asserts has no meaning. Yet it has meaning, and you have encountered it if you have been reading better books than *Easy Reading Made Simpler Than Ever;* and the greater a novelist's awareness of language, of time, and of place, the greater will be his need for a form and a style to capture his mood.

"The habit of expression," Henry Adams observed, "leads to the search for something to express." Habit and search lead to complexity. Complexity, in turn, may shrink one's audience, at least over the short run, but time and labor teach us that Mr. Faulkner's world is not a "private world" at all, but one to which anyone may admit himself if he looks upon reading less as a passive act than as a pursuit requiring the effort of concentration.

The novelist in search of his own best self continues in his conviction. He persuades himself that his defiance of the temptation to increase personal comfort at the sacrifice of craft assures him the distant reward of fame. It is his faith, his religion. He remembers an early day when he was called "promising," and he knows that although he has been moving beyond "promise" his audience has failed to widen. Yet perhaps it has solidified, and he may live to hear, as Faulkner has, the praise of a generation which has discovered that his seeming difficulty is in fact the inevitable result of his ambition to express a difficult idea.

You may not admire Faulkner. You may prefer Hemingway, James, Katherine Anne Porter, or someone else whose ears have grown fantastic big. Whoever it is, if he or she is truly good he is good not alone upon the basis of two or three enduring works but because of his service to a literary principle whose foremost article of faith declares, "I write. Let the reader learn to read." And our best writers are indebted to those readers who by strenuous labor learn to see how those prior references, which Mr. Coughlan cannot locate, are not only present but are embedded in exactly the place—and in the only place—Mr. Faulkner could possibly have put them.

Whether the contentment with easy reading is more pernicious in our own age than it was in any other I do not know. I cannot really think so. People with neither the will nor the means to grow ears have never sustained literature. It is disturbing, however, to discover presumably literate people, some of whom wear the uniform of teachers of literature, who parade secure in the belief that they can read books without *reading* them. They read reviews. They watch television. They will feel confident that they have read *A Farewell to Arms* after they have seen the motion picture produced by Mr. David O. Selznick: he read "résumés of appraisals by book critics."

They say, I cannot understand your book. I think you left something out.

But everything is there. Everything you need to know is there.

I am told, It has baseball players in it.

Yes.

Then it is about baseball.

No.

They say, I see where your book was on television. *Now* you are going places.

But I left nothing out. It is simply that I cannot explain. A novel is drama, not report; scene, not exposition. You will pardon me if, in my obsession with craftsmanship, I cause my people to speak to each other, not to the reader. "Good morning, Mr. Smith, chief engineer here at Atlas Tool Works." When I hear such a speech I will write it down.

I am a storyteller, not a sociologist or linguist or psychologist. I do not educate nor reform. When I am writing my novels I leave my morality in the other room, and I therefore plead with you to differentiate between the characters of a book and the character of its author. Until you appreciate viewpoint you cannot read.

I cannot tell you when to laugh. If you say, "I did not laugh," I can only reply, "Grow ears."

I shall not *tell* you anything. I shall allow you to eavesdrop on my people, and sometimes they will tell the truth and sometimes they will lie, and you must determine for yourself when they are doing which. You do this every day. Your butcher says, "This is the best," and you reply, "That's *you* saying it." Shall my people be less the captive of their desires than your butcher? I can *show* much, but show only, and if you have ears you will do what Mr. Shakespeare and Mr. Hemingway have taught us to do: you will vivify dialogue by setting your own music to the words, bringing to your own reading your own creative intelligence, your own imagination. You will no more expect the novelist to tell you precisely *how* something is said than you will expect him to stand by your chair and hold your book.[1]

I know of no serious novelist now at work who is deliberately mysterious or obscure. If, for example, he distorts time, he does so because his events, he feels, thereby gain force in the telling. The reader who reads will sooner or later see that the novelist has done what he has done for the sake of his story. In conversation we do the same, compressing, rearranging, careless of sequence in the interest of the sharper truth we fashion by dramatizing experience. The novelist's rebellion is not against clock nor calendar but against the form and manner of the novels he has read, and against, most of all, his own last novel. The serious novelist chiefly resists the mixture as before, his own mixture or anybody else's, desiring for his newest work exactly that precious quality heralded weekly but delivered much less often: originality.

Nor will he tell you what his novel *means*. All the actions of life have their themes, their morals, that "natural symbolism of reality" of which Mary McCarthy speaks. A novelist's proper role is only to show an action, or a series of related actions. For people with ears each day, each encounter, each contest of person with person, informs life, and the novelist but extends experience, carrying his reader to new places and to new acquaintance. The symbols await analysis and explication, but this is the work of the reader, not of the writer. You cannot say, "It gripped me, it moved me, I couldn't put it down. What does it mean?" For then you are saying that the writer did his job, but that you have not done yours.

---

[1] In a half-page of Brinkley: "Ensign Siegel said blankly," "Ensign Siegel said absently," "the exec exclaimed," "the exec whipped out," "the exec shouted" ("with a canny smile"), "the exec said ferociously," "Siegel said urgently," then "fervently," etc. —*Life*, July 2, 1956, p. 124.

Preface: Easy Does It Not

"I write. Let the reader learn to read." I must be as skillful as I can. I am obliged to be the best craftsman I can be. I must be free to choose my subject and my language, and I am at liberty to experiment, to grow, to express, if need be, the complexity of my experience with whatever resources are at hand. I will talk baby talk to babies and dog talk to dogs, but I cannot tell you in baby talk or dog talk of the excitement of being an adult human being in a world so wondrous with hope and sorrow and loyalty and defeat and anguish and delight.

All of us who *write* once made the decision to write out the best that is in us. It has nothing to do with Integrity, only with taste and preference. Loath to tape our ears to our skulls, we said, instead, We shall let our ears grow up and away and see what happens.

We want to tell the jokes we want to tell, and we can tell them only to people with ears to listen, people who will bring to the evening talents to challenge our own, who will work as goddam hard to read as we work who write.

The people reign in the American political world as the Deity does in the universe. They are the cause and the aim of all things; everything comes from them, and everything is absorbed in them. . . .

The whole book that is here offered to the public has been written under the influence of a kind of religious awe produced in the author's mind by the view of that irresistible revolution which has advanced for centuries in spite of every obstacle and which is still advancing in the midst of the ruins it has caused.

ALEXIS DE TOCQUEVILLE

Pitching is a most unnatural motion. The shoulder was not constructed to throw a baseball.

DR. GEORGE BENNETT
of Johns Hopkins Medical School,
quoted in Sports Illustrated

SPECIAL SOUVENIR SCORECARD

NEW YORK MAMMOTHS VS. WASHINGTON, AT NEW YORK, JULY 4, 1956
(INDEPENDENCE DAY: DOUBLEHEADER)

CEREMONY

*Martial and occasional music by the All-Boroughs Symphonic Marching
Band:* IRVING PACINI, Conductor.
Our National Anthem: VIVIENNE O'BRIEN. ROSA V. WAGNER, *organist.*
(*The players will assemble and form along the foul-lines.*)

IDENTIFYING NUMERALS, SOUBRIQUETS, POSITIONS, AND NATIVITY OF ALL THE MAMMOTHS

39 SCHNELL, HERMAN H.	"DUTCH"	*Manager*	*St. Louis, 1893*
38 BARNARD, EGBERT	"EGG"	*Coach*	*Philadelphia, 1896*
37 JAROS, JOSEPH T.	"JOE"	*Coach*	*Moline, Ill., 1895*
36 STRAP, CLINTON B.	"CLINT"	*Coach*	*Mason City, Wash., 1906*
13 TRAPHAGEN, BERWYN P.	"RED"	*Coach*	*Oakland, Cal., 1919*
9 BARR, WESLEY H.	"CHOCOLATE"	*Catcher*	*Eugene, Ore., 1937*
16 BIGGS, PORTER L.	"BLONDIE"	*Pitcher*	*Morristown, N. J., 1932*
18 BROOKS, JONAH F.		*Catcher*	*New Iberia, La., 1932*
45 BURKE, LINDON T.		*Pitcher*	*Lusk, Wyo., 1930*
21 BYRD, PAUL R.	"HORSE"	*Pitcher*	*Culpeper, Va., 1921*
5 CARUCCI, PASQUALE J.		*Right Field*	*Port Chester, N. Y., 1923*

6	CARUCCI, VINCENT F.		*Left Field*	*San Francisco, 1925*
46	CASELLI, FRANKLIN D. R.	"F. D. R."	*Pitcher*	*Oakland, Cal., 1932*
48	CRANE, KEITH R.		*Pitcher*	*Wooster, Ohio, 1929*
4	GOLDMAN, SIDNEY J.	"SID"	*First Base*	*Bronx, N. Y., 1928*
2	GONZALES, GEORGE		*Third Base*	*Pinar del Rio, Cuba, 1926*
1	JONES, ROBERT S. (CAPT.)	"UGLY"	*Shortstop*	*Batesville, Ark., 1921*
19	LONGABUCCO, FRANK P.	"LAWYER"	*Outfield*	*Peekskill, N. Y., 1931*
24	MACY, HERBERT	"HERB"	*Pitcher*	*Athens, Ga., 1928*
20	MC GONIGLE, REED		*Outfield*	*New Haven, Conn., 1932*
7	ROGUSKI, JOHN L.	"COKER"	*Shortstop*	*Fairmont, W. Va., 1930*
42	SIMPSON, PERRY G.		*Second Base*	*Savannah, Ga., 1931*
3	SMITH, EARLE B.	"CANADA"	*Center Field*	*Winnipeg, Canada, 1929*
22	STERLING, JOHN A.	"JACK"	*Pitcher*	*East St. Louis, Ill., 1925*
12	TYLER, WILLIS J.		*Infield*	*Dade City, Fla., 1933*
17	VAN GUNDY, JAMES S.		*Pitcher*	*Central City, Nebr., 1932*
25	WHITESIDE, JOHN J.	"WHITEY"	*Pitcher*	*Dublin, N. H., 1936*
44	WIGGEN, HENRY W.	"AUTHOR"	*Pitcher*	*Perkinsville, N. Y., 1931*
23	WILLOWBROOK, GILBERT L.	"GIL"	*Pitcher*	*Boston, 1929*
10	WOODS, THURSTON P.	"PINEY"	*Catcher*	*Good Hope, Ga., 1935*

PROBABLE STARTING PITCHERS (figures in parentheses indicate Won and Lost record as of Monday night, July 2).

FIRST GAME: Van Gundy (9-5) or Wiggen (15-1) vs. Walter (The Wizard) Womack (11-5).

SECOND GAME: Wiggen or Van Gundy vs. Harold (The Mouse) Littleman (6-6).

NOTICE TO PATRONS: *Fireworks are prohibited by Law.*

THE SCHEDULE (*continued*)

15 NY at Phila, thus concluding the exhibition season, or "Grapefruit League," commenced at the Southern training base of The New York MAMMOTHS, *Aqua Clara, Florida; Mon Apr 16 Open Date.*

Championship Season: Tues Apr 17 Bos at NY (Opening Day, Ceremony); Wed Apr 18 Bos at NY; Thur Apr 19 Bos at NY; Fri Apr 20 NY at Wash; Sat Apr 21 NY at

Championship Season: Tues Apr 17 Bos at NY (Opening Day,

The hotel was freezing cold. I told **Piney** tell somebody send up some heat when he went for the mail, but he either never told anybody or else nobody listened. Who listens to Piney Woods, a kid, 20, fresh up from Queen City and greener than spinach? He come in again with the mail in his hand, all for me and none for him, and I leafed it through with one hand, blowing on the other all the while, Holly's letter, and some insurance matters. I sell insurance, mostly to other ballplayers, keeping out of the poorhouse that way. I got insurees on every big-league club but Kansas City, for we never hit Kansas City. I also glanced over the fan mail, and when I was done I shoved it in a big envelope which about once a week I ship the envelope

3

up to Holly, and she writes these little notes, "I thank you for your friendly letter and for your interest in my work," and sends them back to me to sign. The postage is tax-deductible, business. The least I can do is *sign* them I guess, though some people think I'm out of my mind answering my mail. I don't know.

The only thing I didn't shove in Holly's envelope was 2 postals from my regulars. They always come on days I work, one from a fellow in Bloomfield, N. J., saying "Luck to you and every member of THE NEW YORK MAMMOTHS," and one from a fellow in Astoria, Long Island, "I hope you blow higher than the sky, you phoney."

This particular day there was also a very thick letter from a girl out West that I didn't have time to read but tossed on the dresser and went in and run hot water in the tub and left the steam drift out and maybe warm the joint up a little. "Whitey Whiteside says it will be called on account of cold," said Piney.

"Green punks passing along rumors to green punks," said I.

"You got time to give a glance in that letter from the girl out West," he said.

"I am trying a little thinking," said I, "plus also

keeping from freezing to death at the same time. Does it never strike you as a good plan to try a little thinking about a ball game beforehand?"

"It is nowheres near freezing," he said. "Freezing is 32°." Piney got a very scientific mind. "I will open it for you."

"Freezing is how you feel. I *feel* freezing no matter what science predicts."

He slit the letter open with a knife he bought on Broadway, 8 blades, $4.98, a corkscrew, a nail file, a bottle opener and what-not else, plus also a little tweezers you can shove through your shoe and grab the lace when the end snaps off in case it goes against your principle to buy new laces. He later forgot the knife by accident in the hotel in Cleveland and felt extremely blue for about 35 minutes. "Here she is," he said.

Up in the corner of the letter was this $10 bill sowed to the paper, and I run my eye up and down Page One to see if it said what for, but there was no mention. It was a very long letter covering her whole life history it looked like, and her mother and her father and her brother and her sister as well, and her town, and the history of the town, and the new building—The Federal Mart, they call it—which her father and her brother laid the bricks

5

one Summer. It now looked like I was to be told the history of each and every brick, and I took it over and laid down and begun reading. She had the most marvelous handmanship. You would of thought it was wrote by machine, very tiny but yet very easy to read, and Piney laid down on his bed with his feet on the wall, for he got this scientific theory if he lays on his back with his feet on the wall he saves wear and tear on the blood vessels of his legs, which maybe he does and maybe he doesn't for all anybody knows. He lays like that for hours, studying his wall all hung with his guitar and his motorcycle and his drawings of naked girls and his reservation to the moon. Piney can draw like a mad fool. I'll say that much for him.

I read through Page 2, passing each page across to Piney when I was done, and there was still no mention of the $10, and then the phone give a jingle, and it was Dutch. "Time," he said. He makes you ride to the park with him days you are scheduled to work. It ain't too terrible. I threw the letter back on the dresser and grabbed my coat. "You better wear a coat," I said to Piney. "Go turn off the tub."

"Who needs a coat?" he said.

"You do," I said. "Because it is *freezing*. And leave that letter lay exactly where it is."

6

"Mind over matter," he said, and he wore no coat but grabbed the letter instead. You might as well been talking to the door. He read the letter walking down the hall, and when the elevator opened he walked right in, still reading. George Gonzalez was in the elevator sniffing through one of these gadgets that clear your nose, for he caught a cold coming North, him and ½ the club besides, and we said "Buenos dias" back and forth a couple times, me and George. George pointed at Piney's sweater, for that was all Piney wore, a little yellow sweater that you could see clear through, and I shrugged my shoulder, and George took the gadget out of his nose and pointed it at his head, like a gun, same as saying, "Piney is out of his mind."

"Where is Red?" I said.

George took the gadget out of his nose again and run it up and down his cheek making a noise like an electric shaver, and then he put it back in his nose and we piled in Abe Silver's cab and waited. Dutch got to have Abe and nobody else. "Hi-ho," I said. The boys all call him "Hi-ho," or sometimes "Honest Abe." "Hi-ho, Silver," I said, "I hope you brung your snow chains."

"It is cold," he said, "but no snow predicted according to the radio. Cold or not, Author, you never

7

been troubled by Boston." It is what people call me, due to the books I write. I am the only baseball player that ever wrote my own books to the best of my knowledge. It is something to do over the Winter and keeps me out of the poorhouse besides. Red Traphagen finished shaving and come along a minute later all bundled up in this very warm jacket saying "S. F. State" on the front, which is where he teaches over the Winter, English, however, which I doubt you need the jacket for. But I ask no questions unless invited, believing in minding my own business when possible.

"Hi-ho, Silver," he said, and Piney got out and left Red in, for Red must sit in the middle. George flipped open a jump-seat and blabbered at Red in Spanish. "George says turn on your heater," said Red, and Abe turned on the heater.

"A girl that can write this small," said Piney, "and yet give you every word clear as a bell has probably got a mighty sharp pair of eyes."

"Or she might wear glasses 3 feet thick," I said.

"Who is this?" said Red. He lit up his pipe.

"A girl out West," said Piney. "A seamstitch. I wish she sent on a photo, for I believe she is a beauty."

"A seamstitch is libel to have round shoulders,"

8

said Red, "and her hands are libel to be all full of pinholes and such."

Piney was through Page 4 by now, and he passed them to Red. "Give me your opinion," he said, for he got only the greatest respect for Red, Red from Harvard and all, and Red read a page or 2 and squinted up his face some until finally he flipped back to Page One and seen where the letter was mine in the first place, not Piney's, the 2 of them sitting reading my mail which I hardly got past Page 2 myself so far.

Then soon Dutch come out the hotel pulling on his gloves, and Piney got out of the cab and left Dutch in, for Dutch must sit in the back. "Howdy, Mr. Schnell," said Piney, and he jumped back in and flipped open the other jump-seat, and we took off.

"Hi-ho," said Dutch, "turn up your goddam heater."

"It is already up," said Abe.

"Fine heater," said Dutch.

Abe begun discussing certain problems concerning his heater, which I suppose I was the only individual listening, Red and Piney reading the seam-stitch's letter, and Dutch thinking, and George not understanding the language, Dutch cutting Abe

9

short in the middle, saying, "If you gentlemen **can** tear yourself free from your literature I got here **a** couple interesting statistics," and he fished his glasses out of one pocket and polished them on his sleeve and set them on his nose, and a handful of these little scraps of paper, and he pawed through them. But he liked none of them, and he rolled down his window and fluttered them out, all but one, and he rolled the window up. "According to this," he said, "Boston beat us 7 times last year, 3 of these times due to the result of not pitching in the correct manner to Kussuth. Outside of Kussuth I got no respect for anybody on Boston. To me, Boston is nobody." He snapped his finger. "We must simply never throw him fast-balls."

"I never do," I said. I never do, neither. I throw him curves, slop, junk, anything but fast-balls, anything but speed, and I usually never have trouble with Kussuth nor all of Boston.

"It is simple science," said Piney. "Who but **a** stupid child would throw speed at power? You must force an individual like Kussuth to manufacture his own power."

"Very good thinking," said Dutch. "I call it common sense learned over the period of $\frac{1}{2}$ a century.

10

Call it also science if you wish. It means no speed at Kussuth either way."

"½ a century?" said Red.

"40 years and more," said Dutch. "You might as well say ½ a century. It is a long time. It is 41 Opening Days. My first Opening Day we was at war since the previous Thursday. We was never sure if we would open. But we done so."

"It is both a long time and a short time," said Red.

"What war was that?" said Piney.

"It was cold," said Dutch. "I hit 4 for 2 off a right-hand pitcher name of Aloysius Shannon, an Irishman, the first ballplayer I ever seen wear eyeglasses. You see many nowadays. And every Opening Day colder than the one before."

"I remember it was cold in 52," I said. "I remember Red caught me and I was scared out of my skin." It was my first start, Opening Day, 1952. The following year Red went off the active list.

"You ain't lost an Opener," said Dutch. "You been a good boy over the years and a pride to my heart."

"I ain't scared," said Piney. "I ain't got a nerve in my body."

11

Tues Apr 17

Dutch took off his glasses and polished them on his sleeve and stuck them in his pocket, and Red and Piney whipped out the seamstitch's letter again, George sniffed away at the gadget, and Abe took up the problem of the heater where he left off, though I doubt anybody was listening but me. I mean, you can't just leave a person talk and not *listen.*

The park was 750 times colder than the street, a stiff wind in from center, but low. A high wind, OK, for it hurts the hitter, but a low wind is no pitcher's wind.

I don't think I warmed proper. First off I couldn't find a catcher. We carried 5 catchers at the time, Piney plus Jonah Brooks plus this bonus baby name of Chocolate Barr that we was required by law to keep or else lose, plus 2 other kids that I forget their name, one shipped back to the farm at Queen City soon after and the other swapped to Pittsburgh for 75 quarts of liniment everybody said. It was what he was good for. Piney was in the cage, for he rather hit than warm, and Jonah was also in the cage—*ordered* to hit, though he rather warm—and the other 3 were wandering

12

around like a chicken out of water looking in the wrong place for the right thing to do, the first time any of them been in a big-league park in their life until finally Red looked my way and seen what I was up against and grabbed a mitt and warmed me. I hurried.

"Do not hurry," said Red. "Slow, slow, slow, slow and easy does it every time," and I slowed a little. The boys finally chased Piney out of the cage and he come down and took over for Red and warmed me about 30 seconds until he decided Red's mitt was no good, and he went back for his own, me standing there in the wind, nothing between me and Alaska but a barb-wire fence until Red come back again and warmed me some more until Piney Woods finished 4 different conversations between here and the dugout. Then Piney took over at last, and Red stood beside him and told him a thing or 2, and then he strolled down my way— Red did—and watched me, and he said, "That was a most marvelous letter from that seamstitch when you stop and think about it."

I said I didn't even read it yet so couldn't hardly stop and think about it.

"Consider the honor," he said. "I was never

13

much the hero of the girls myself. Maybe my hair ain't the right color. You are working up a little sweat at last."

"She ain't sinking yet," I said. "She should of begun sinking by now." My fast-ball will not sink until I am warm. If I am not warm, or if I am tired, my fast-ball won't sink. It is the sure sign.

He walked around and watched me from the other side awhile. "Remember what Dutch said concerning Kussuth," he said. "As much as I do not like the man I also admire him. ½ a century is a long time. Of course, what she is really looking for is a husband. Make Piney go down in the dirt." I threw a couple low and sent Piney down in the dirt. "Make him go down in the dirt backhand," said Red, and I done so, and Piney scooped a couple out backhand. "Knock him down," said Red.

I let fly at Piney, full speed. But she did not sink. After the first one Piney took his sponge out of his pocket, and when he done so a whole raft of papers fell out as well and begun blowing all over the place, and he chased after them, the pages from the seamstitch, and the clucks along the fence sent up a howl while he chased around stepping on the pages and picking them up and putting them together by the numbers and folding them over and sticking them back in his pocket, and the clucks all clapped and cheered, and Piney touched his hat, and Red laughed, and I would of laughed myself if my jaws weren't all froze together again by now, and I threw a few more and we went back in for Dutch's lecture. It was warm inside.

Then afterwards there was the ceremony, and the flag went up, CHAMPIONS OF THE WORLD, for we were, hoisted up the pole by yours truly (Most Valuable Player, 1955) with the help of a cluck holding the lucky number on his raincheck. *"Snowcheck* you might as well call it," said I to the cluck, and he got a great laugh out of that. The Mayor then heaved out the first ball, the boys all scrambling for the ball until Piney finally come up with it and jigged over to the Mayor's box for his autograph, and he said something to the Mayor that sent him off in a fit of laughing—the Mayor, not Piney, for Piney never laughs—and they stood around discussing matters. I got my hands on a ball and chased Chocolate Barr out of the dugout and made him keep me warm until Piney and the Mayor finished solving all the problems of the City of New York. The Mayor was wearing about 19 scarfs around his neck.

· · ·

15

Tues Apr 17

It was so cold I almost forgot to rub my letters until the clucks all begun shouting, "Rub! Rub!" I rubbed them then, the letter *W* and the letter *E* on the front of my shirt, though nobody knows why, only me and Holly, and the clucks all clapped and sat back, and I touched my hat, same as saying "Thank you for reminding," and Winter was over all of a sudden.

Aleck Olson opened for Boston with a little hopper down the first-base line that Sid grabbed easy enough and flipped to me, covering. "The dividends begun," said Aleck. "Good," said I, Aleck an insuree of mine, his first dividends now begun, and he jigged on back to the Boston dugout. I begun thinking maybe I could get warm before I met trouble, but I didn't. I lost Buddy West, which I shouldn't of. But I thought I better not bring the fast-ball in yet, not sure if it would sink, and Buddy seen the curve kept missing the corner, and he waited me, and I lost him and went to work next on this kid name of Rolly Schnell (no relation to Dutch), a right-hand hitting third-baseman fresh up from the Boston farms with a great reputation in the newspaper. I worked somewhat careful, for we had no book on him yet and no information to go by. He kept

16

measuring the fence with his eye. I tried the fast-
ball, but it did not sink, and he knocked it between
George and Coker into left, Buddy West holding
second out of respect for Vincent Carucci's arm.
Vincent actually had a sore arm at the time, but he
threw good in drill, one long heave for show, and
Boston was none the wiser. Whitey Whiteside begun warming in the bullpen.

The boys all gathered around, and Piney come
down from the plate, and we talked the situation
over, and then what we done against Kussuth we
pitched the first pitch outside and wide, and Piney
whipped it down to Perry at second, and Buddy
West went sliding back in, and then when he got
himself dusted off he led off again, and I wheeled
and threw back to Perry again, and Buddy went
sliding back in again, safe again, and got up and
dusted himself off again. I toed in. Then I stepped
off and stared at Buddy West awhile, and Coker
dashed in behind him from short, and West hugged
up, and Dutch yelled from the bench, *"Keep* that
runner close down there," all of us putting on the
most terrific act in the world, like Buddy West was
worrying us sick. We should of all went on the
stage and become rich.

I pitched again, ball 2, wide, a gamble. "Gambling is winning," says Dutch. "Playing safe is second-division." And Piney took the wide pitch and begun his throw, looking towards second, only instead of throwing to second he threw to first, looking at second but snapping the throw to first, like Red drilled him all Spring coming North, Sid moving in behind Rolly Schnell and taking the throw and slapping the tag on the boy, and Schnell was dead before he knew what happened, his jaw hanging open standing flatfoot watching for the action at second base, him and all of Boston and 12,000 clucks and the Mayor of New York besides no doubt. I laughed. Anyhow, that opened first base, and we put Kussuth on, and the fast-ball begun sinking a little now, and we pulled out of the inning OK, no damage. Whitey Whiteside sat down in the bullpen.

It was Piney drove home our first run. Canada drew a walk to open the second, and Vincent Carucci moved him along, and Piney slammed one back through the box into center. He was hitting in the 7 spot in front of Coker. Piney is a sweep hitter they call them. He aims at the pitcher's hat. I hate that kind. There's a kid on Brooklyn name of Sal Wilhelms that shouldn't worry me any more than the peanut hawk except he aims his drives down through the middle and a couple times damn near took my hat off, not to mention my head for a bonus. This is the kind of a hitter Piney is, a sweep hitter, that a pitcher throws outside to and sometimes loses. Piney draws many a walk, and Dutch puts Coker in the 8 spot, backing Piney with power. He made his turn at first base, his buttons all busting, his first big-league RBI, and he took off his helmet and threw it away and pulled his hat out of his pocket, and when he done so the seam-stitch's letter come fluttering out and flying all over the grass. The clucks all roared. The umps called "Time!" and Piney and the Boston infield and Clint Strap—Clint coaching at first—they all chased around every which way gathering up the pages in the wind, and Piney put them back in his pocket, and Dutch yelled down to Clint, "Clint, take his goddam literature away!" and Clint done so, and Dutch went muttering up and down the dugout, "Running around with his pocket full of paper, running around with his pocket full of paper!" Piney never wore a helmet ever after.

I was warm by now. I pitched 3 really good innings, 2-3-4. I got past Kussuth again in the 3rd, striking him out with a curve, Piney first calling for speed, his mind on other matters by now, but I shook him off. Sid hit a home run in our ½ with Perry aboard, a nice clout that bounced around in the empty seats near the bleacher gate and sent 100 clucks racing down the aisle after the souvenir. Some poor pitiful fellow took a spill and got stampeded on, and the first-aid wagon went in action, the fans all making a noise like a siren, like they do, but he was not hurt bad, nothing much, according to the paper.

Piney told me Dutch had no legal right ordering Clint to take the seamstitch's letter, robbing the United States mail was what it was, Piney said, and I told him calm down and keep his mind on business and Clint would give it back, which he done. I mean, Clint later give it back. I was sweating excellent by now, but I was tired, and I went back in the clubhouse and told Mick give me a Despadex. The clubhouse was all in a fog. Mick had the steamkettle plugged in, and about 4 of the boys were sitting around breathing up steam for their cold and watching the TV. Horse Byrd was laying in the tub trying to soak out this hamstring muscle he pulled in Savannah coming North. Mick give me only ½ a Desdapex, however. "It is false pep," he said.

"False pep is better than none," I said, and I went back out. The reason I was tired was I warmed too much in my opinion, wore myself to nothing trying to beat the cold. I give up a run in the 5th, though I got past Kussuth again.

I got 2 men out in the 6th and thought I was free and clear, nobody left to face but Toomy Richardson, the Boston catcher, a fellow that in 4 years never hit as many as 2 doubles off me, strictly no hitter. One time I told him, "Toomy," I said, "I believe I could handle you with my right hand," which I believe I could if I really thought about it much. It is always good seeing Toomy up there. We generally throw him speed, and he grounds to George or Coker, or sometimes if he ate his Wheaties in the morning lifts a lazy fly out Vincent Carucci's way, so I threw him speed, like always, and it never sunk, and he powdered it. It kept rising. It popped against the upper deck in left and fell to the ground, and Vincent picked it up and wiped it off and tossed it in the visiting bullpen, and Toomy touched all the bases on the way around, and he called to me, "Author, try me right-hand next time."

Yet it was our ball game still, 3-2 going into the 7th, and I begun writing the headline, AUTHOR WIGGEN WINS 5TH CONSECUTIVE OPENER IN A ROW and figuring on dinner with the boys and calling

Holly, for I always call her when I win. When I don't win I don't call anybody, and I rather eat alone. If you talk to anybody they say, "Well, you can not win them all," which happens to be the one remark in the English language that rubs my goat the wrong way. Only then I never got a man out in the 7th. I lost Buddy West again, and this kid Rolly Schnell singled, his second hit off me that day, and I am sure he rushed back the hotel afterwards and whipped off a letter like a green punk will do, "Dear Mom and Pop, I guess I am up here for life. This big leagues ain't hardly as advertised," though by June we had a pretty good book on the boy, and by August he was no doubt writing home to his folks see if that slot was still open coaching all sports for the "Y". Good field, no hit, like in the old saying. Dutch come up out of the dugout, and the boys gathered around. " I warmed too long," said I to Dutch.

"There should be a law against playing ball in ice and snow," the boys all said.

"Maybe so," said Dutch. He spit. "Yet Boston seems to manage," and he give the wigwag for Whitey Whiteside, and Whitey come in from the bullpen, and I give him the ball. Dutch said to Whitey, "I trust you are warmed proper."

22

"Certainly," said Whitey.

Certainly! Green punks are always warm.

I wiped off the TV screen. It steamed back up again. "Tough luck," the boys all said, and Mick brung me a cup of coffee and I told him what I thought of his Despadex, and I loosened up my pants and sat on the edge of the tub with my feet up and watched Whitey go to work on Kussuth. Horse was still laying in the tub, and I wished it was him out there saving my ball game instead of Whitey, Horse the best relief in the business, bar none. I hope when I am 34 I got Horse's arm.

Whitey threw Kussuth speed! I looked away.

When I looked back the TV was kind enough to show me where my ball game went, up in the seats in Section J. There is a spot in the stands shaded off maybe 15 feet from the left-field pole which even on your biggest days is the last place to fill. Don't ask me why. I went up there once and sat, and it seemed like good seats to me. The office been trying for years to figure it out. Everybody calls it the cemetery, for nobody wishes to be in it. The clucks are mysterious and no mistake. The TV showed them racing down the aisle after the souvenir, and then it switched and showed Rolly

23

Tues Apr 17

Schnell and Buddy West shaking hands with Kus-suth, Schnell and West charged against me, according to the TV. Hot news!

"A green punk flashing signs to a green punk," said Horse. "It makes your hair boil." The TV now showed a shot of Piney down in his crouch, the whole screen practically nothing but Piney's rear end. Sensational view! "It is where his brain is," said Horse.

Holly called, and Piney picked up the phone and said "Howdy," and I told him give me the phone and stop running up my bill. It was the first word I spoke to him since supper, and I didn't speak to him at supper neither, for I ate alone. I read the seamstitch's letter at supper which I got back off Clint, the pages all covered with dirt and spike-holes from Piney and the Boston infield. I leaned it against the sugar until the waiter come and grabbed the sugar out from under. I bawled him out proper. Then I left him a big tip, $1. "Howdy," she said.

"Howdy," I said.

"I polished off the income tax," she said. "Michele got a cold," Michele my daughter, born the day of the All-Star Game, 1955, and named in honor of Mike Mulrooney that managed me at the Queen City Cowboys.

"We played baseball," I said.

"So I seen," she said.

"Everybody got colds," I said. "I got a very interesting letter from a girl out West. She is throwing up her job and coming East by the 4th of July." The 4th was my birthday, 25, ¼ a century.

"Maybe she will do your income tax for you," said Holly, "and nurse your baby through her cold, and write your letters to your fans, and keep on top your insurance matters, and polish up the grammar in your books, and live alone all Summer."

"What else is new?" I said.

"Well," she said, "today I been repairing the furnace."

"It is cold down here as well," said I.

"I had to laugh at Piney losing his papers in the wind," she said. She kissed me in the phone a couple times.

"I do not consider him a laughing matter," I said. "That was that letter."

"Might be you can work up that girl from the

West's interest in Piney," she said, "seeing you already got a girl."

"Might be," I said.

Piney went for the paper and the late mail, and I kissed her in the phone a couple times, and we said this and that, no need repeating, and when he come back I read the mail and the headline. It made me mad—the paper, I mean—and I crumpled it up and slammed it in the basket. I wasn't in too good of a mood.

"The trouble is," said Piney, "she ain't sure she got the money to get her here by the 4th." He laid on the bed with his feet on the wall drawing pictures. I said nothing.

"If I owned a wad of money," he said, "I would send her some."

I said nothing again.

"In the meantime I am a little short to payday," he said. "Maybe you could loan me a couple dollars, Author."

"Meaning what?" I said.

"About 50?"

"No," I said.

"Here she is," he said, and he passed across a drawing of a very beautiful girl, and I give it a glance and passed it back, and he hung it by fric-

26

tion on the wall. I can not do it myself, but Piney can, rubbing a hunk of paper down the wall like you might rub out a splotch of these Gerber Junior Baby Food that my baby heaves against the wall all Winter, and slapping it on the wall so it hangs by friction. I tried 750 times to work up the friction like Piney does, but I simply can not achieve success.

"Here is who?" I said.

"The seamstitch," he said.

"I will tell you a secret," I said. "The top artists often take a look at what they are drawing before they draw her."

"Mind over matter," he said. "I know a seamstitch down home is one of the most extremely beautiful women I ever had the honor meeting."

"Many more stunts like today you will soon be down home all right," I said. Piney is from Georgia, a place by the name of Good Hope. I never been in Good Hope. I been in 45 states plus Mexico, Cuba, Japan, and Canada, however. I picked up the letter and snipped the threads where she sowed the $10. The reason she sent the $10 was she wished a seat in a box on the third-base side for the 4th of July, if she made it. She was bound and determined to make it, mad for baseball and mad for yours truly besides. It was like a dance, she said, and she done a lot of dancing whenever she could break away. The boys all said she was the best dancer in town back home. I stuck the $10 in my pants and folded the letter over a couple times and threw it at Piney, and he opened it up and flattened it out and hung it by friction, 13 pages.

"How many acres in the park?" he said.

"750," I said. I didn't know how much an acre was and still don't. She said she could never get a very exact picture of the park in her mind because she never seen it referred to in acres, only in city blocks. "250 acres down, 250 back, and 250 across." I said.

Piney laughed. He never smiles, but he might sometimes laugh, and then when he does he bites it off quick for fear you might catch him at it. "You hand me a laugh," he said. "An acre ain't long nor short, but square."

"Shaped like the head of Piney Woods," I said.

"I wonder does she mean the park itself or the seats included. It is easy enough to calculate by science if I once knew the facts and figures. 750 acres! Ha! Why, 750 acres would stretch you clear off the island."

"What island?" I said.

"Why, the present island," he said. "The one you are situated on."

I guess I knew but never thought about it much. I never get the feeling I am on an island. What difference? With 750 tunnels and bridges leading out it's the same as dry land as far as I can see, and I said so, and he laughed again and bit it off short again and found a fresh place for his feet on the wall.

"I will send her the measurements pronto," he said.

"You got no right encouraging her," I said. "Her father and her mother and her brother and her sister are against it. How will she get far without money? She will be dead in a ditch by the road. What will she live on once she manages to arrive? You got no right."

"Work her way," he said. "Then when she gets here work some more. Gamble. This is a first-division girl through and through."

"According to who?" said I.

"According to her own personal letter," said Piney.

"She is one more cluck," I said.

"What you got against clucks?"

"Nothing," I said, "which is why I hate seeing

them dead in a ditch and broke in New York."

"I will send her the measurements," he said, "and I will also buy her the ticket. Hand over the $10."

"No," I said.

"You got to either send her the ticket or her money back," he said.

"Do I look like a thief?" I said.

"You might forget," he said. "It is an obligation."

"I never forget money," I said. "Nor another thing I never forget is I never forget what I am told about any particular hitter, such as you were told concerning Kussuth by me and Red and Dutch. You have simply got to apply your mind to things."

"I got it on things," he said.

"On too *many* things."

"Listen here, Author," he said, and he rose up on his bed. "I will not be told by you nor anybody else what things I must keep my mind on and what things to keep them off of. It just simply happens that I am the kind of a man that got his mind on more than one thing at a time." His face was all tight and tense. "I have not got a single-track mind like you that if I call the wrong pitch and pull a rock I stew and sweat and call myself dirty names and shiver for fear Mr. Schnell will eat me out and wish the day I was born was tore off the schedule at birth and throw the newspaper down on the floor and tromp all over it because it carries the bad news." If his face went any more tense he would of been smiling.

"Yes," said I, "you got many tracks on your mind." I got up and slipped in my shoes. "I only wish there was somebody at the switch," I said, and I took off.

Where I went, I went all over the cockeyed hotel hunting up somebody to go to the Automat with. This seamstitch kept talking about the Automat in her letter. Outside of the ball game it was her greatest ambition in New York. We always ate in the Automat in 52, me and Coker and Canada and Perry and Squarehead Flynn, the 4 of us fresh up to the big time, greener than spinach from the Queen City Cowboys in the 4-State Mountain League. We all stuck, all but Squarehead, still back on the Mammoth farm in Queen City and probably for life, though a finer fellow never lived. Canada and Coker only laughed and sneered when I mentioned it now. The colored boys were playing cards, Perry and Jonah and Wash and Keith. "Too busy," said Perry, never looking up, and Red was reading a book and hardly looked up neither, and George I would of went with if we could of talked, but he knows 5 words in English and I know 6 in Spanish and it don't make for many topics, so what I finally done I started out all by myself.

It was cool when I hit the street, and I buttoned up the top of my shirt. But it was still cool, and I went upstairs again and slipped in a jacket, and I said to Piney, "How about the Automat?"

"Not if you go like that," he said, "without no tie."

"It is a very scientific restaurant," I said.

"No," he said. He was still laying on the bed reading the seamstitch's letter on the wall. "I wish she sent a photo," he said.

"Have it your way," I said, and I hopped in Abe Silver's cab. "Hi-ho, Silver," I said, "take me to that Automat over down Broadway."

"Tough luck, Author," said Abe. He flipped his meter. "I just this minute carried Dutch home from class." Dutch was taking this class in Rapid Reading at The Institute of Rapid Reading, trying to keep on top scouting reports and such. "You cannot win them all," said Abe.

"How many acres from here to the Automat?" I said.

He thought this over for about 2 lights. "It is anybody's guess," he said. "$1.05 by the meter maybe. What is up?"

"Nothing," I said, "but I just got a memory of chicken pie reading a letter mentioning the Automat."

"Who goes $1.05 down and $1.05 back for chicken pie, $2.10 round trip? What is wrong with the hotel?"

"Down there they get their chicken straight off the egg-plant," I said.

"Author," said he, "never mind the jokes tonight, for I ain't in too good of a mood. I am worried this kid Whiteside ain't got the promise as advertised."

"Maybe it was somebody else's fault besides Whiteside," I said.

"Then tell Dutch get at the root of the matter without delay."

"You just seen him," I said. "Why did you not tell him yourself?"

"I would of," said Abe, "only he did not seem to be in too good of a mood."

It was the same old Automat. It was warm in

there, and good. I ate chicken pie and milk sitting swung around facing the door. I watched the people come and go, and the more I watched the worse of a mood I got in, all these people drifting in and out and counting their nickels, and tomorrow the same thing over again, 5 days per week, 50 weeks per year, maybe 12 hours a day like Abe, 5 times around the world per year without ever leaving Manhattan. One time in 1939 he carried a fare to Baltimore and never forgot it. Yet you will hear no complaint from Abe. These people, probably they never rode a cab from one year to the next, probably wore a tie though it choked them, probably never went farther than Jersey, much less 45 states and 4 countries, Mexico, Cuba, Japan, and Canada, and I said to myself, "Is there a one of them spent their Spring in Florida over the Winter? Is there a one of them got $10 in the mail today? Is there a one of them anybody's hero like I am that seamstitch's hero? They get bills and taxes in the mail, and they are a hero to their wife, maybe, or their kid, or their dog."

They should of been in 750 times worse of a mood than I was. Yet many were laughing. And my *own* face was all frowning, and it struck me if you was to walk in the door that minute and glanced around—if you was somebody sharp, a private eye or a writer or somebody—and your eye was peeled for the most miserable face in the crowd you would point at me, and you would say, "How come so miserable?" and I would say, "I draw $40,000 per annum plus twice drew a full share of the Series melon, 52 and 55, $15,000 plus change, less taxes, plus royalties off books plus commissions off insurance plus endorsements off 16 different products plus TV spots now and then, so why I am miserable is I lost a baseball game today." And you would say, "Then you are out of your mind, and a weak sister besides. You ain't got ½ the courage of Abe Silver. For here is a whole Automat full of clucks, and many are laughing, while you got a frown from ear to ear on your $40,000 face. You ain't got 6% the spirit of a cluck." I wouldn't of minded. It was true.

Soon a very beautiful girl come in, and I watched her go the rounds. No harm in watching, that's my motto. She bought cherry pie (3 nickels) and coffee, and she looked for a place to sit. She seen my opposite seat was empty, and she looked at me, and I at her, and she drifted over and sat and folded open her paper and ate her pie and read about the ceremony, this Grace Kelly and the prince. The

headline said MAMMOTHS DROP OPENER, WIGGEN
ROUTED. GOLDMAN, KUSSUTH, RICH'SON HOMER. A
couple times she looked in my face like she knew
me, and then down where my necktie wasn't, like
she would know me if I only had it on. "Tiepockets," I said. "I am a victim of this rage of tiepockets going on that you been reading in the
paper."

"Tiepockets," she said. "Yes." She looked down
at the paper. "So far I ain't got much past Kelly
and the prince these last couple days."

"Converted pickpockets," I said. "Like in football they convert an outfielder to a pitcher, such as
they done with Babe Ruth."

"You mean *baseball*," she said. "Plus which it
was the other way around what they done with
the Babe."

I snapped my finger. "I always get them mixed.
What season is it now?"

"Baseball," she said. "They just opened today.
Brother, do not talk to me of baseball. Baseball is
where my summer and my pocket money goes,
for the so-called man that I married must witness
one baseball game per week when the Mammoths
are in town. 750 years ago he played second base for
the Manhattan High School of Aviation Trades

and never leaves you forget it. It is now down to where I either leave him flat or go back to earning my own pocket money."

"Stick to the man," I said.

"I suppose I will."

"Make him take you along."

"He does. It is the only relief I get. At least at the ball game you know where you are at, yet sometimes I wish it would rain all summer, buckets and buckets, never stopping for 40 days and nights from Opening Day till October."

"Sometimes I wish the same," I said.

"At least at the ball game you find out," she said. "Who is playing? Look at your schedule and see. Who bats after Canada Smith? Look at the board and see. Who just done what? Look at your scorecard. Check his number against the card. Do you know what I do? He says to me, Check that man's number against the enemy card, and I sit checking while he watches the action. The world's fool. Will Sid Goldman hit more home runs than Kussuth? Who will win the duel between Author Wiggen and Walt Womack the Wizard of Washington? Was he safe or was he out? Look at the umpire and see. How many consecutive games in a row did Joe Di-Maggio hit consecutively in? Who holds the record for the most times smashing their head against the wall? Who is DiMaggio to me? I wish they would all smash their head against all the left-field walls from here to St. Louis."

"It never rains 40 days," I said.

"It might. It been known to happen."

"I rate Wiggen over Womack," I said.

"Yes," she said. "I thought you would, for I know who you are all of a sudden, too. You are him. Lord, my heart! Henry the Author Wiggen! I did not mean you, I mean I meant all the rest of them, not you, I mean concerning smashing their head against the wall. Sign something! Please, for I know you are you. Please! Please! Here, on the paper, over Kelly and the prince of Monaco. Here, too," and she fumbled in her bag. "My husband would murder me. Here, sign my Social Security. Here too. He would murder me, absolutely murder me," and I signed on the paper and her Social Security and also on an envelope, writing "To friend So-and-So," whatever their name was.

"1,000,000 thanks," she said, and she looked at the little scraps of paper I signed on, and she smiled at them like they was 3 winning tickets to the Irish Sweepchase, and I said, "Now, Honey, wait a minute, for I will sign you something proper and not be all in a rush. These are warm-ups," and I went to the girl in the money window and told her hand me a decent hunk of paper, and she fished out a hunk, and I went back and sat down and wrote out this girl and her husband a whole long message. I covered the whole paper, front and back, how we met in the Automat eating cherry and chicken pie, and I wrote the address of the Automat down, and the date, Opening Day, 1956, and my autograph, Henry W. Wiggen, "Author," which is what everybody calls me.

emony); Wed Apr 18 Bos at NY; Thur

Horse Byrd was jigging around in little circles down the left-field line still working out this hamstring muscle. I was shagging flies. "Where is your pal Piney Woods?" he said.

"Pal?" I said.

"A man better be a pal to his roomie," said Horse. "It is a long Summer, and getting longer every year."

"For all I know off to the moon," I said. Piney bought this reservation to the moon, $50.

But I could not laugh it off so easy, for what Horse asks he hears from Ugly Jones—Ugly the Mammoth captain—which Ugly hears from the coaches, Joe Jaros usually, and which Joe hears straight from Dutch 9 times in 10. Certain people

40

carry around Dutch's questions until they are answered, and some don't—Red don't—and you do your worrying according to what line of people the worrying follows. So I begun worrying, not wishing Piney to get eat out. Yesterday was yesterday, and he is my roomie besides, for better or worse, like they say. I glanced around here and there and everywhere for Piney, but I did not find him. "He got a little cold in his nose," I said. "No doubt Dutch give him the day."

"No," said Horse, "for it is Dutch been doing the looking," which was what I was afraid of. I really begun glancing around like a madman now. I located every catcher but Piney. He was nowheres, not in the cage and not warming anybody, and nobody was on the bench, neither, nor at the bubbler, for Dutch was at the bubbler and everybody was drilling and trying to look busy if they could.

"Back off a way," said Horse, "and tell me how my motion looks," and I backed off a way, still glancing all over, and he threw a few, still leaning light on the hamstring, trying to get back over as fast as he could on the healthy leg.

"You are delivering quick," I said.

"Shut up," he said. "Do you not think I know it?"

Wed Apr 18

"You told me tell you," I said, still glancing.

"I am cold and stiff and crowding 35," said Horse. "The sun is still cold. Not 2 weeks ago, on this very ground we are situated on, it snowed. I am no April pitcher any more." All the way in to the lecture he told me the various troubles of old age. I did not see Piney.

I changed my shirt and sat, and the boys gathered and the writers cleared out, and F. D. R. locked the door as soon as everybody was in. F. D. R. got this superstition he will put the whammy on himself if he ain't the man to lock it. We waited. If things went good yesterday it is a very pleasant time, too. Dutch will come from the conference, him and Red and Clint and Joe and Egg, the coaches, the brass, and sometimes Ugly, too, all of them laughing, and you know the lecture will be sweet. There is 2 lectures, one marked "Sweet" and the other "Sour." Yet you can never be too sure, for if the sour treatment don't work there is the sweet, too, even after a bad day. He suits the treatment to the need, so you never really know until they come from the conference. If they come quiet, none of them laughing, no sound but their spikes on the floor, and Dutch whistling between his teeth, you know you had best climb under the woodwork if you can. The sure sign of danger is Dutch whistling.

This particular day he was whistling "I Wander Today To The Hills, Maggie, Where You And I Were Young" plus "I Will Be Down To Get You In A Taxi, Honey" plus "3 Little Words" all mixed in with strains and scratchings from a number of others, and he stood on the scale a minute, which is where he stands, and he looked us over like we was a collection of the 2 dozen fattest and homeliest girls in the world before breakfast, and he stopped whistling, and he said in a quiet voice, "Where has Piney Woods wandered to?"

Nobody knew, and he whistled some more, and he said, "Author! Where is Piney? The truth. Do not cover."

"I do not know," I said.

He begun whistling again, "Marching Through Georgia," and he took off his hat and studied it. 40 years with the same club, going on 41, ½ a century you might as well say, he still got to *look* at his hat. He should of went on the stage and become rich. "It says the letter *M* on my hat," he said, "but it is hard for me to believe after what I witnessed yesterday that it stands for Mammoths, for what I seen stood for Mediocre plain and simple, or

43

Mickey Mouse maybe, or dancing round the Maypole bush or the prince of Monaco, but it did not stand for Mammoths." Red does a very comical imitation. Private performances only. "Nor it did not stand for Money," said Dutch, "which very many afternoons like yesterday mean nobody in this room now wearing the letter *M* on their hat is libel to find in a World Series envelope when October and the melon rolls around. All yesterday I looked at the pole and seen a flag marked CHAMPIONS OF THE WORLD, but then I cast my eye back on the criminal procedures going on under my gaze, and I said to myself, Go dial the police because that flag is not there by rights nor honest effort but been *stole*. Boys, I am not a young man much longer. Do you wish me to bear such a feeling on my shoulder?" He touched his 2 shoulders. "Do you?"

"No sir," we all said.

"You, Roguski, do you wish me to bear such a feeling?"

"No sir," said Coker.

"Yet yesterday you run the bases like a drunk. Pasquale Carucci, I fell off the bench in shame and surprise seeing an experience hand like you laying clear out on the clay against that joke of a lad. Who was that lad?"

"Aleck Olson," said the brass.

"Aleck Olson that ain't drove a ball so far in his life except on his birthday more than 3 times a year."

"I am sorry," said Pasquale, and he bowed his head. Vincent Carucci bowed his own head, brothers. Next to me, Red was putting it in Spanish for George, and George was listening and studying.

"Jonah Brooks will catch in the place of Piney Woods," said Dutch. "Piney been summonsed elsewheres than here this fine and pleasant afternoon. We made the little mistakes, but it was Piney actually done the murder, which I warned him concerning Kussuth, and Red warned him, and Author warned him no doubt, but I might as well been talking to the bubbler. His mind is in the hemisphere. Roguski hit 7. Jonah, you hit 9 behind the pitcher. I have spoke to him both in private and ate him out in public, and I wrote both his father and his mother. I believe a wife might solve him, but while waiting for a wife to show her face I must figure out another means of throwing fear in his heart. I do not know. Any observations?"

45

"The outfield is wet and slow all over," said Canada.

"Good observation," said Dutch. "Pasquale and Vincent, did you hear?"

"Yes sir," they said, and they raised their head.

"Some boys do not answer to fear," said Red.

Dutch stuck his glasses back in his pocket and thought over what Red said, and he whistled some more, "Marching Through Georgia" still, mixed in amongst "Baby Your Mother As She Babied You, Back In Your Baby Days," and then he stopped and all was silent. He looked at the clock.

Then Piney himself banged on the door. Nobody opened it. "Open the door," said Dutch, and F. D. R. reached over and opened it, and Piney rushed in all breathing and scooted across to his locker and tore off his clothes, and nobody spoke a word, Dutch whistling a little and squinting at the clock again. "You are one hour and 25 minutes late," said he, "which figuring 60 minutes to the hour at $1 per minute, which is by no means the salary paid in the fields and farms of Good Hope, Georgia, I fine you 60 plus 25 equals $85. Does that check by your clock, too, Piney?" Everybody laughed a little, for Piney got a watch showing 24 hours instead of 12, and he took it down off the shelf and looked at it.

"Yes sir," he said, "it checks out. I did not know it would take so long. I asked Mr. Jaros." He was all naked by now.

"You asked me nothing," said Joe. "I never in my life give an individual permission to miss drill and doubt that I ever will."

"I only went up front and bought a ticket and told the girl send it to this girl out West," said Piney to Dutch. "She wrote asking to reserve one in a box for the 4th of July. But she did not have the measurements." He was standing on one leg slipping in his stocking.

"The girl out West?" said Dutch. "Did not have *what* measurements?"

"No, the girl up front," said Piney. "Mr. Jaros give me permission to ask up front for the measurements. She wishes to know them."

"*What* measurements?"

"The measurements for the girl out West," said Piney. "But she did not have them."

"The girl up *front* did not have them."

"Yes sir, so what I done I took the measurements myself and give them to the girl up front and told

47

her shove them in the envelope with the ticket. Mr. Jaros said it was OK by him."

"For all I cared you could took the measurements of the Statue of Liberty only so long as you was back on the job for drill was what I said," said Joe.

"Advance forward and tell us," said Dutch, and Piney advanced forward and stood all naked in the middle of the room, one stocking on. "What was you measuring? Was you measuring the mileage to the moon?"

"I was measuring the park," said Piney. "I measured the grass and I measured the seats. I do not know which she wishes, so I sent her both."

"As regards this girl out West," said Dutch, "she is who? A girl you met in Queen City or where?"

"I never met her," said Piney.

"By correspondence only?" said Dutch.

"Yes sir."

"Is she much of a looker? Is she wife material?"

"I ain't ever exactly seen her," said Piney.

"By photo only?"

"No sir, not photo neither."

"A surprise package," said Dutch. "Well, they sometimes turn out OK, too, I guess, though I rather not run the gamble if I was a young man any more. How high is the grass? How wide are the seats?"

"No," said Piney. He tip-toed up on the bare foot a little, for the floor was cold, and somebody threw him a towel and he said "Thank you kindly" and put the bare foot down on the towel. He looked only at Dutch. "No, I measured the length by the width, first down on the field and then in the seats. It was measuring the seats took up the time with the clucks all filing in."

"Is the job complete?" said Dutch.

"It is 5 minutes of," said Egg to Dutch.

"Yes sir. I multiplied the measurements and calculated the square and divided by square paces per acre to come up with the answer in acres like she wished."

"Like the girl wished out West," said Dutch.

"Yes sir. I am glad you got it clear at last." He hunched up his shoulders a little, for it was cold. Somebody threw him a jacket. Somebody then threw him a hat, too, and everybody laughed a little, not much.

"It sounds scientific all right," said Dutch.

"The reason I measured by paces," said Piney, "Mr. Traphagen says it is the way men been measuring since the good Lord laid out the Garden of

49

Eve, so I figure it is scientific enough for me." He got a great faith in anything Red might say, Red a teacher by Winter in the college in San Francisco.

"But he did not say measure during drill," said Dutch. "If you took him so serious on the subject of measuring by paces why did you not take him serious when he told you never sign for fast-balls at Kussuth? You cost us the ball game. I ain't heard many kind words said concerning you the last 24 hours."

"I am afraid of nobody," said Piney, and he give us all a look, the first time he looked any place but Dutch. "I called for a fast-ball at Kussuth earlier in the ball game, and Author shook me off. Why did Whitey Whiteside not shake off my sign?"

"Because Author is an experience hand in these matters. You can not expect your pitcher to be doing your concentration, in particular a young lad fresh up like Whitey Whiteside. Now," said Dutch, "as a method of improving the concentration of Piney Woods we will place him in permanent charge of the enemy bookkeeping until he mends his way. You will also look for your sign at Piney, seated on the bench in the place of honor. The sign for today is as follows. Piney digging in his left ear will be the sign for sacrifice, Piney digging in his right ear the sign for bunt and run, Piney digging in his opposite ear with his right hand the sign for hit and run, and Piney digging in his opposite ear with his left hand the sign for steal." He begun whistling again.

"It is a minutes of," said Egg to Dutch.

"I am done," said Dutch. "There would be no such a delay but for the like of Piney Woods. Go slip in your clothes, Piney, seeing if you can concentrate. Your hat goes on your head and your pants go on your hip." Blondie Biggs give Piney the enemy book, and Piney picked up the towel from under his feet. A pitcher usually always does the bookkeeping, usually the pitcher next in rotation. Some boys complain about the bookkeeping, but I do not mind it a-tall. It is educational and worth the work.

We straggled on out down the alley, Piney hustling along soon after, buckling his belt with one hand and the book with the other, and he sat down beside Dutch on the bench, and he done the bookkeeping and flashed the signs Dutch told him, and I sat beside him, keeping my eye peeled on him for fear he would dig in his ear by mistake—not signing but only itching—and send the boys running at the wrong time. "Do not worry about me, Author," he

51

said, "for my mind will conquer matter," and I said I hoped so and believed so, but I kept my eye peeled all the same.

We squeezed it out, 5-3, Van Gundy going all the way for us until finally needing a little relief from Horse in the 9th. Our power was off, both the Caruccis still looking for their eye, which they later found as soon as we faced the West, but in the meantime the power was off and getting no charge from the bottom end of the order, mostly due to Jonah, and I know this worried Dutch. Still and all, games won is games won, the only news better than rain, and everybody was soon in a better mood than yesterday.

F. D. R. beat Boston again on getaway
day, a nice job, complete, 7 hits. Sid hit 2 home
runs and a double, 6 RBI, which I told him I
wished he done Opening Day and saved me my
ball game, and everybody got a great laugh out of
that. F. D. R. should of worked Opening Day in
my opinion. He was the readiest. He won his next
5 starts as well before coming down with an elbow
following the swing West in May, 6-0 on his Won-
and-Lost. Yours truly also won his next 6 starts,
and also went on and won a considerable number
besides before anybody blew the whistle on me. It
is all history now. Yet no harm in mentioning. We
run into weather all through April, and we passed
the colds around from nose to nose. But we was
all in a good mood.

Thur Apr 19

Me and Piney ate dinner and went up and begun packing for Washington when right in the middle Dutch walked in whistling "Oh I Come From Alabama With My Banjo On My Knee" between his teeth and sat down and crossed his leg over the other and sat studying Piney's wall. Piney had her letter hung, but from right to left instead of the general way. Don't ask me why. Dutch got up and begun reading from the left before seeing the light, so he then went down and begun at the other end, and Piney said, "Mr. Schnell, I would appreciate you not consulting my private correspondence," and Dutch said "Just whatever you say" and went and sat back down again. "What will the hotel say when they see you been plastering their wall?" said Dutch.

"It is not plastered," said Piney. "It is hung by friction."

"I admire your science," said Dutch, "and I wish to compliment you on the way you flashed the signs today and done the bookkeeping. You will find it improves your concentration. Are you finished the sum and totals?"

"All but the paper work," said Piney. "I plan on finishing up on the train."

"Good boy," said Dutch. He crossed his leg over

the other again and give us a few more moments of "Oh I Come From Alabama With My Banjo On My Knee" and looked out the window some. I finished up my bag and rung for the boy, and we sat on the bags waiting.

"Mr. Schnell," said Piney, "I hope you do not mind me criticizing you, but about ½ the time you whistle flat."

"Was I whistling?" said Dutch. "My mind is far away worrying. What I been worrying over is I think I might of been a little stern and harsh on you in the clubhouse, due to the fact of not being in a very good mood. I am slicing your fine in ½, $42.-50, call it 40 even. Yet I know that you know that what I done I done towards a good purpose, not for the purpose of throwing fear in your heart, for in my opinion you are not the kind of a boy that answers to fear, but for the purpose of learning you your job, for your own sake and the sake of the club, and help you develop the kind of a one-track mind necessary to fill your promise. You got in you the making of a 285 hitter and a first-class catcher. In ½ a century in baseball I think I speak from experience. I seldom been wrong, as the record will prove. You know, Piney," said Dutch, "I was 38 years old and managing this present ball club the day you suckled your first, September 18, 1935, according to the book, a Wednesday doubleheader vs. Cleveland. We split. I was a few years later elected, an immortal enshrined, a statue of my bust in the Hall of Fame in Cooperstown, N. Y., yet as for you you was still playing choose-up on the playgrounds of Good Hope, Georgia."

"I am not afraid of you," said Piney.

"A good spirit," said Dutch, and he whistled but soon stopped. "I hope you ain't going to tell me the banjo is also hung by friction."

"Guitar," said Piney. "No sir, it is hung on a nail which was already there in case the hotel wonders, and the motorcycle is hung by glue, all the rest by friction." The motorcycle was quite huge, Piney in his helmet and goggles and a girl on behind. The name of the motorcycle is Good Hope II. The name of the girl he don't remember. Dutch made him leave the motorcycle home in Georgia.

"Why would not a fast little car serve the purpose," said Dutch, "and keep you in out of the rain and be quieter and probably even safer besides?"

"I seen a fast little car made in Europe that some clucks give Mr. Ted Williams, does 125 M. P. H. and only 38 inches high," said Piney.

"Why not buy it?" said Dutch.

"It cost $25,000," said Piney.

"Why not start a savings?" said Dutch.

"I could save," said Piney, "if Author would leave me take a vacation from insurance, which every time I turn around he loads a new protection round my neck." I might of sold him a little insurance at that. In the long run he will thank me. "It is draining my life," he said.

"How much did you plunge on the reservation to the moon?" said Dutch.

"$22.50," said Piney.

"Covering everything?" said Dutch. "Covering meals and extras and tips and baggage?"

"Plus tax," said Piney.

The boy come for the bags, and we all stood up, and Dutch looked at his watch and begun walking around the room. I sat down again. I figured if I missed the train I was in good company. It cost you $25 fine to miss the train. "Are you not afraid these young ladies might catch their chill?" said Dutch. "Who learned you anyhow to draw? These are mighty fine, and I hope you will keep it up, for art is a great thing and safer than motorcycles."

"I learned myself," said Piney.

57

Thur Apr 19

Dutch glanced over all the drawings. "I am not reading your private correspondence," he said. "I am only admiring these ladies. Well! Well," he said, "look at here! Here is a real beauty only she forgot to leave her duds behind. Yet I guess a young lady would look mighty out of place playing the organ all naked at that."

"She is on a sowing machine," said Piney. "She is that girl out West, the seamstitch."

"Then she sent on a photo," said Dutch.

"No sir," said Piney, "not yet."

Not yet! She *never* sent on a photo.

"Wife material," said Dutch, "for I remember when I was a young man I seen all the girls naked except the girls I thought might serve as a wife. Such as my Mrs. She looks like 40,000 stars of stage and screen—your drawing, I mean, not my Mrs. any more—though my Mrs. was a looker herself not long ago, the prettiest girl in all Missouri, or anyhow such was my opinion." He begun whistling "The Missouri Waltz" between his teeth mixed in with odds and patches of "Meet Me In St. Louis." "She weighed 117 the day we was married. We was married by Andrew Hayden, a first-baseman for Philadelphia, though he did not last once the lively ball come into use. He went back to his

58

church work. I seen him only a couple years ago."

"She sure put on weight over ½ a century," said Piney. "My trouble is I got to practice clothes. I do not draw clothes too good, not having much practice as yet."

And we locked up and started down the hall, and when we got as far as the elevator Dutch said, "Piney, I will make you a fair and square deal, for maybe I was too stern and harsh calling thumbs down on the banjo and the motorcycle both. If you will promise me no more cowboy music which drove me out of my mind last year I will call thumbs up again on the banjo. But you must promise me your concentration will improve."

"Guitar," said Piney, "yes *sir*," and he run back for the guitar and caught up with us in the cab. "Hi-ho, Silver," said Dutch. "Away."

THE SCHEDULE (continued)

June 13 NY at Chi; Thur June 14 NY at Chi, thus concluding the second Western tour.

At Home: Fri June 15 Pitts at NY (Night); Sat June 16 Pitts at NY; Sun June 17 Pitts at NY (Doubleheader); Mon June 18 Open Date; Tues June 19 Chi at NY (Night); Wed June 20 Chi at NY; Thur June 21 Chi at NY; Fri June 22 Cleve

At Home: *Fri June 15 Pitts at NY (Night)*;

She run out of money just the other side of
Queen City, a wild little town name of State Line
that me and Perry and Canada and Coker and
Squarehead Flynn went down one afternoon and
lost our pay at the hand of the gambling machines,
back when we played under Mike Mulrooney for
the Queen City Cowboys and he polished the green
off us, and we all stuck, all but Squarehead. The
bus driver said to her, "Honey, it is 30 miles from
State Line to Queen City, which at the rate of one
kiss every 10 miles I will carry you there for 3
kisses," and she give him the 3 kisses, and he said,
"I wish we was a transcontinental bus."

Or anyhow that's what she wrote in the mail,
the first word I heard except only this postal the

day she left home. The postal said, "Thank you for the ticket and the measurements, and *here I come.*" On the other side was this corny photo of The Federal Mart all retouched by a photo retoucher like they do. I use to know this girl in Queen City, a photo retoucher. I forget her name. THE FEDERAL MART, said the photo, HOUSING U.S. POST OFFICE, U.S. AGRICULTURAL INFORMATION OFFICE, U.S. RECRUITMENT AND ENLISTMENT OFFICE, U.S. SOCIAL SECURITY OFFICE, AND U.S. INCOME TAX SERVICE. Service! Sensational service! She drew a little X on the sidewalk, for it showed where she would be standing and waiting for the bus, and her father and her mother and her sister and her brother went with her this fine and pleasant May morning and seen her off. They all said to her, "Honey, stay home. You will never make it," but she stood firm, and they seen that she meant what she said.

She pulled a rock in Nevada. Every place the bus stopped she fed a little change in the gambling machines, not much, she said, but some, enough, and she lost more than she won, which I could of told her if I knew she was going through Nevada. I lost $200 passing through to the Winter leagues in Mexico in 53, none of it deductible on your in-

64

come tax unless your winnings equal or exceeds your losings. Service. Rushing you in the poorhouse is a service all of a sudden. She cashed in what was left of her bus ticket in the depot in Winnemucca, and she put a notice in the local paper there, MENDING DONE BY THE DAY, giving the number of a pay phone, and a gambler called, saying, "Come up my hotel, Honey, and patch my duds," and up she went and sowed everything in sight, sitting sowing by the window. The gambler sat across from her running "21". When he beat himself he give her a smile, and when he lost he swore. When she was done she said, "$6, please."

"$6!" said the gambler. "For that much work? It is an insult."

"I am a top-flight first-rate seamstitch," she said, "and that is my prices."

"I will tell you what," said the gambler. "How much is the bus to Queen City? Double or nothing, high card. Draw!"

"It is a good deal more than $6," she said.

"Draw!" he said. "I will run the risk."

She drew a 3. "That ain't bad," he said. "You got the making of a gambler," and he shuffled the deck a bit and drew a deuce, and he bought her the ticket to Queen City, all for nothing but patching up his duds. She climbed on the next bus out of Winnemucca and she escaped Nevada, except they stopped for dinner in State Line, 30 miles the other side of Queen City, and she took courage from what the gambler said, believing maybe she had the making of a gambler after all, so she played the machines in State Line, and she went broke again, and she cashed in the rest of the ticket, and she played the machines again. And she went broke still another time. Yet she made it **OK** to Queen City, 3 kisses was all it cost her. She planned on hitting Queen City broke anyhow.

The letter was on the stationery of the Blue Castle Hotel in Queen City, the rest on paper borrowed off The Geographical Center of the United States Motel (The Largest Scientific Accommodations and the Softest Beds in America). It took all afternoon to read. I laid on my bed and read it and passed it sheet by sheet across to Piney.

"Do you not feel like 1½¢ worth of hamburger giving her the impression it was you that sent the ticket," said Piney, "and you that sent the measurements by acres, when the plain fact of the question is it was me that sent them and got eat out for my trouble and fined $40 besides leaving me broke to payday?"

"Not especially," I said.

"Maybe you could loan me a couple dollars, Author."

"Meaning what?" I said.

"About 50?" he said.

"No," I said. "Set her right," I said.

"I damn well will," he said, and he took his guitar off the wall and begun thumbing a song name of "I Damn Well Will (at Bunker Hill, 1775)," chorded for guitar in a book of songs he bought in St. Louis, PATRIOTIC HYMNALS, TUNES, AND BALLADS. Then all the way back from the West no matter what you said to anybody they answered you back, "I damn well will." Once Piney starts a song there is never any stopping it, for it drives you out of your mind. You whistle or you sing, or else you just stand still and leave it run round and round your brain, like in a bad dream you stand still on the hill and see enemy runners running round and round the bases, and you pick up the words, and all the boys the same, and the brass as well, and Dutch. Last year it was cowboys out of a book of cowboy songs chorded for guitar, and everybody begun saying "Howdy" and "How are things back on the ranch?" and this year it was patriotic hymns, tunes, and ballads. It begun in the West and never quit.

Coming back from the West everybody was in a good mood. The base hits begun falling for the Caruccis once they found their eye, and the sun warmed up. We seen the circuit round, and we seen where Washington would be the club to beat, and we knew that we could beat them, too. We all got a great laugh seeing in the paper where a cluck in Virginia bet a fellow on 134th Street 12 hams against a suit of clothes on the outcome, for we could see him licking his tongue all Winter over the ham, the fellow on 134th Street. "You could at least send her back her change out of the $10," he said. "She needs it worse than you."

"Here," said I. "Send it!" I wrote him out a check for $6.85. "I got a wife already and a child besides, and for all I know another on the way," another child, I meant, for Holly stood in New York for a week in May and believed she might of become pregnant at that period, but Piney said "No! I will not be caught touching her money."

"No need to touch it any longer than to shove it in the little old envelope," I said.

68

"Never mind," he said, and he thumbed another tune, "The Cornwallis Surrender Country Dance (Carolina and Virginia)," which we sung in Perkinsville when I was a kid to the tune of "Pop Goes the Weasel," and what I finally done I stuck the check in the mirror in the bath. But Piney never touched it, and neither did I. It stood in the mirror until the 3rd of July.

She said everybody in Queen City was worried (this was still on the Blue Castle paper in May) but she believed the Caruccis would soon find their eye. She said everybody said if it wasn't for yours truly Henry Wiggen we would of been in a real flounder. She stood at the hotel with the club —the Cowboys—and Mike Mulrooney bought her dinner the first couple nights, and Squarehead Flynn bought her breakfast in The Wild West Brick Oven where me and Perry and Canada and Coker and Squarehead always ate because they served Perry there, no questions asked due to his color, and she liked Squarehead OK once she got use to him drinking one bottle of Coca-Cola with his grapefruit and another with his eggs. I had forgot about that. She said it must be quite a considerable strain on me and F.D.R. lugging the whole club all through the West on my one left arm, though actually it was no strain a-tall. It is what I am suppose to be paid for when the need rises. I am the Number 4 man on the payroll, second only to Sid and Pasquale Carucci and Ugly, and I would probably equal Ugly except he draws this little bit extra for being captain, $500.

I was carrying the load all right at that. I beat Washington the first weekend we left home, and I beat them again back in New York towards the end of the week. It looked like I was the only individual could beat the son of a bitches. I also beat Pittsburgh and St. Louis in the West and shut out Cleveland. I was 5-1 on my W-L, which looked good enough to me by the middle of May, plus which the power went on by now and we was neck and neck with Washington and everybody was in a good mood.

In Queen City she put a notice in the paper, MENDING DONE BY THE DAY, taking her calls in Mike's room in the Blue Castle, where many a long afternoon I sat and listened to tales of the olden days. They play strictly nights out there. Finally a call come from a lady give her a bundle to sow, and she done such a first-rate job she got about 7 calls the following day, and she took the ad out of the paper, and all week she worked, and after the ball game she hung with the boys. She showed them the ticket for the 4th of July, and then she sowed it back in her blouse, and she took a room with a very fine view of the mountain, and she slept like a stove. The only thing bothered her sleep was in the middle of the night the boys all come banging on her door, wishing to discuss baseball, they said, she said.

There is an old superstition that the club on top on the 4th of July will win the flag. This been true 36 times in 55 years, 65.4545% of the time, she said, and Piney checked her calculation out and said the same.

She believed that when she hit New York the 4th of July we would be on the top of the heap for good, though everybody said to her, "Honey, turn back! Go home. You will never make it." She would make it, she said, come hell or hot water.

"Too bad about the catching," she wrote.

"What is too bad about what catching?" said Piney.

"She wrote this beforehand," I said. "Read forward."

"She damn well did," he said.

Well, she said, luckily a good pitcher don't need

to worry about the kind of a catcher he got, any cluck can catch. With luck, she said, she might even get to see me Tues-Wed-Thur June 5-6-7 in St. Louis, though meanwhile she was still back in Queen City fighting off the Cowboys banging on her door and sleeping and rising at the first sight of dawn coming over the mountain and sitting by the window and sowing on a poem she planned on sending me when done. She hoped and believed I would like it, she said, for it would be in red and blue, the same shades as the Mammoths home colors, one word red and the next word blue, and all on a sea of white matching the shade of a base-ball Mike give her, a very precious baseball that the Mammoths give Mike after the last game he ever played. Mike hands out about 9 a Summer. "So what?" says he. "So it makes an individual happy and none the wiser," and what Mike finally done for her he said to the boys, "Boys, with a little co-operation we can get this fine lass up over the mountain at no extra cost," and the boys all said, "Sure, Mike," and she left with them on get-away day, and they smuggled her on the train and over the mountain as far as Denver.

And in Denver the boys all said to her, "Honey, stick with us and see the circuit round. What has

New York got that the 4-State Mountain League ain't got? Baseball is baseball.''

"Yes indeed," she said, "baseball is baseball. There are 100's and 100's of baseball players in all the 48 and spreading like wildflower to other lands besides, but there is only one place called the Big League. Then too, there are 400 ballplayers in the Big League but only 25 called the New York Mammoths. And amongst the New York Mammoths there is only one left-hand pitcher name of Henry Wiggen.''

"So who is Wiggen?" said one of the boys. "He was once only a Queen City Cowboy himself." She didn't say who said this. Still and all, it is true. You might as well face it.

She stood firm, and Mike seen that she meant what she said, and him and Squarehead piled her in a cab and carried her out East Colfax Avenue, out past Aurora where I once knew a girl that I took to the amusements at Elitch Gardens when it rained. I forget her name. It hardly ever rained when we were in Denver. They carried her out to where the highway splits, and Mike stood on the highway and flagged down cars. "Which way you headed?" said Mike to the driver, "the North road or the South?" He believed it was best she took the

73

Fri June 15

North through Omaha, and if the driver was headed North he looked him over, Mike did, and decided if he looked reliable and wouldn't take advantage. "Are you married?" asked Mike. "Do you have children? Do you indulge in alcoholic spirits excessively? Do you live in one place or do you float? Do you go to a church? Was you ever arrested for any crime higher than traffic?"

"Drat Mike anyhow," said Piney. "Why has he got to be so particular?"

"Stay calm," I said. "Read forward."

She run out of the paper borrowed off the Blue Castle Hotel in Queen City and now begun using The Geographical Center of the United States Motel paper. Piney tried the Blue Castle paper for friction, and it stuck. Some type paper won't hang by friction no matter what. Don't ask me why.

"Hurry it up," he said, and he went back and laid down again, and Mike finally flagged a fellow down married with 3 children, a job, a church, no arrests, and never a floater. "Good luck," said Mike, "and say love and luck to the boys up in New York. Tell Author never mind busting Hubbell's record, only play for the sake of the club," meaning Carl Hubbell. I now won 8 consecutive games, 8-1 on

74

my W-L, and I was hot, and the paper begun playing with the idea I might bust Carl Hubbell's consecutive record, 16 he won in 1936, an immortal now enshrined, a statue of his bust in the Hall of Fame in Cooperstown, N. Y., and a grander fellow never lived. He sent me a wire July 3, which I saved and keep yet, though there was times through June when I wouldn't of especially drowned in tears if I never heard the name of Carl Hubbell again—when you could not step out the door without some cluck roaring up telling you where you stood in connection with Hubbell, and sending you charms in the mail, everybody in the world pulling for you and wishing you luck, meaning well, no doubt, but adding only tension—or anyhow everybody but this cluck in Astoria, Long Island, "I hope you lose to Hubbell, you phoney." They also called him King Carl, and The Meal Ticket. She threw her bag in the back and hopped in the car and started out the North road towards Omaha.

But no sooner was Mike and Squarehead's cab out of sight than he turned around and started out the South road instead. "Suppose I was to left you back there and some floater give Mike a song and a dance," he said. "Sticking with me I will guaran-

75

tee you get through to New York for the 4th of
July, and I will swear this on a stack of Bibles
when we get to Georgraphical Center, for I own a
regular stack of Bibles there, and I own the Motel
besides."

Well, she said, OK. No man would of swore out
such a promise unless he meant to kept it, she said,
and they drove along. Now and again they come to
a sign saying 150 MILES TO THE GEOGRAPHICAL
CENTER OF THE UNITED STATES MOTEL, or however
many it was, and he stopped the car and out he
jumped and studied the sign, and if it was wrecked
by rain or wind he mended it with paste, and after
a time she said, "You are getting weary. Leave me
paste up the next, working in rotation like they
do," and she done so, and he said, "You are a
mighty capable little girl, not to mention a beauty
besides. I will make you a fair and square deal.
Tell me, when will the Mammoths be in St. Louis?"

"Tues-Wed-Thur June 5-6-7," she said.

"Very well," he said, "you can do us a little
seamstitching around the Motel the next 3 or 4
days, following which I will run you to St. Louis. I
can always mend the COME BACK AGAIN
signs while we go and the mileage signs on the
way back. Maybe the boys will smuggle you on the

train East like they smuggled you over the mountain."

OK, she said, a fair and square deal. She was very fond of him, she said.

"The trade rips up the sheets mighty bad," he said. "It will keep you busy."

"I sow fast," she said.

They pulled in The Geographical Center after dark and ate in the Motel restaurant, all hung with maps proving it was The Geographical Center after all no matter what anybody thought otherwise. There were maps on the napkins and matchbooks as well, and on the wall of the room they give her, Number 48, the furthest room but with a very fine view of the swimming pool. She no sooner slipped in bed, however, than this same fellow come banging on the door, the owner, saying he wished to discuss a matter with her. "I just slipped in bed," she said. "I ain't got a stitch on."

"She wears no pajamas," I said to Piney.

"Well, slip in something and open up the door a minute," said the owner, and she hopped out of bed and slipped in her robe and opened up the door, and he rushed in, him and his wife and their 3 kids, a stack of Bibles in his arm, and he set them on the dresser and slapped his hand on top.

Fri June 15

"God and my loved family my witness," he said, "I will guarantee you get through to New York for the 4th of July."

In the morning she seamstitched the sheets the trade ripped up, and she borrowed a bathing suit off a star of stage and screen passing through and went swimming in the pool. She didn't say who. It was hot out there. She dragged a lounging chair in the shade and sowed on the poem until it was just about ready for the mail by now, long ahead of schedule, she said. But once she was done with the poem there wasn't much doing except dodge the trade. It was really disgraceful, she said. She could barely walk down the drive without some cluck snapped up his window shade and went "Pssst! Pssst! Hey there, Honey!" until she finally told the owner he might as well give her something to do as long as she wasn't doing nothing.

He thought it over. "Well," he said, "go place a Bible in Number 23 and 34 where they been swiped from," and she done so, but it hardly took 5 minutes. Afternoons or evenings she caught a ball game on the radio if she could, or the TV. She was delirious the way the catching squared away by now, Piney Woods back in the lineup since

Memorial Day. A couple more years polish and seasoning would do it, she said, and take the green off him.

"Listen to who is calling the kettle green," said Piney.

But mostly it was a bore, she said, for she was the kind of a girl with more pep and energy than she could use. The idea having nothing to do put her in a mood.

However, one Sunday night the condition changed. The owner said, "Honey, me and the Mrs. been considering. Why not me and her run to St. Louis and you keep an eye on things? We got a great faith in you."

"You swore on a stack of Bibles," she said.

"Swore what?" he said. "I swore I would guarantee you get through to New York for the 4th of July, which I will because I swore it. As far as St. Louis goes, consider me and the Mrs.! Once school is out and the summer trade comes hot and heavy every which way we will get no sleep from one end the day to the other. What kind of a life is that? Sometimes I wish the country run out of gasoline."

"They would figure out something else," she said.

"Sometimes I wish trees sprung in the middle of every highway," he said.

79

Fri June 15

"Then they would chop them down again," she said.

"I guess so at that," he said. "What chance does the Mrs. ever have to get out of the sight and sound of children?"

"None," she said.

"Damn him," said Piney. "Damn him! She might of showed in St. Louis June 5-6-7. Now I doubt she will make it by the 4th neither. Damn his soul, anyhow, holding the girl a slave."

"So I will write you out a little list of instructions," he said, and he done so, and she sent them along as follows.

Sleep in Ofc. Stick colored folks in 47 and 48 up to 4 P. M. Hold reservations up to 5. After that every man for himself. Switch off the neon at daylite. Wake the cook and handy man. Carry the keys on your person at all times. Shovel fresh gravel over the oil spots when the trade moves out. Get the kids to school. Feed the dog. Order food and Coca-Cola. (Keep the machines loaded) Fish foreign matter out of the swimming pool. Get the maids and waitresses on the ball. Mend sheets. Replace Bibles and stationery. Check around. Keep after the cook and maids. Feed the kids and make them do their home work. Switch on neon at dark. If it flutters switch it off and on again.

80

Keep trying. It will catch. Be courteous to the trade. No reduced rates. No refunds. Use great caution in cashing checks. Advise them no parking on the grass. (Water it) When full switch on No Vacancy. Send over flow bound west to The Adobe Abode, 69 mi. bound east to The Rest Of Your Life Motel, 25 mi. Tell the trade to advise them it was our recommend. Put receipts in paper bag in the air condition (over the desk in Ofc.) Put the kids to bed. Lock up. Plumber phone 116, electric phone 215, law phone 100, fire phone 200, hospital phone 300. In case of emergency we will be at the Hotel Mark Twain, St. Louis, phone Garfield 1-4300. Take things easy.

It wasn't much once she got the hang. She met many people and liked them, and the owner and his wife went on to St. Louis and back and seen me win Number 10 the afternoon of June 7. They held their breath the last 3 innings, she said, but I got through, thanks to the power, and she figured I would cop Number 11 as well in Chicago, which I done the first night there, Chicago always a soft touch for me, and she said no doubt their message got through, and then when she said it I remembered some cluck left a message, "We are all thinking of you and pulling for you back in The

81

Fri June 15

Geographical Center," which the switchboard sent
up the room in St. Louis. But I had no idea at the
time she was in The Geographical Center, and I
don't know what in the world I could of done if
I did. It was just another message from another
cluck, no name and no return address, and I threw
it in the basket like you do. I was 11-1 on my W-L
when we come back East. We was 2½ games
ahead of Washington.

Now that they were back from St. Louis she
might as well stay until around the 4th, she said.
He would buy her a plane ticket or else find a party
going straight through to New York, somebody
that looked reliable and wouldn't take advantage.

It all hung by friction, and Piney walked back
and forth and thumbed his guitar, and then he said,
"Hand me a hunk of paper, Author. Make it 2 or
3 as long as you are up, plus an envelope and an air
stamp," and I done so, and with pleasure, too, and
he sat and wrote a bit and then went over and
glanced at the 2 letters now on the wall, reading,
then writing, then thumbing, reading, writing,
thumbing, and when he was done he shoved it in
the envelope and sealed it and stamped it and tore
it all up and threw it in the basket. He left. I fished

the corner of the envelope out of the basket and soaked off the stamp in hot water.

"Where he went, he went and borrowed the dictionary off Red, and when he come back he threw it towards me. "Leave us whip this out in a hurry," he said. "We will set that girl right as quick as we can. Where is the goddam *i* in *deceive?*"

"The *e* before the i," I said. "Deceive. To mislead, delude, cheat, beguile, to lead away or frustrate, usually by underhandedness, to impose an idea or belief contributing to a person's bewilderment or helplessness or make him further the agent's end."

"You needed no help from anybody's agent," he said. "Point One, the great Henry Wiggen never sent you the ticket but left it for me to do. Point 2, never even sent the change. Point 3, never sent the acres but left it for me to do, which cost me $40 fine. Point 4, in a sour mood on losing days, takes credit for winning, blames others for losing, a tightwad, a bad dresser, and a one-track mind." He wrote awhile, and then he sat back and read what he wrote. "Hand me an envelope and an air stamp," he said.

"Send it special besides," I said.

"I damn well will," he said, and he wrote SPE-

CIAL DELIVERY on the outside, and we bought
a stamp to cover it in the lobby, or anyhow yours
truly bought it, for Piney was a little short change
at the moment, and we mailed it on the way to the
park.

at NY; Thur June 21 Chi at NY; Fri

That was a Friday. The following Thursday
the poem come. I think it was the following Thursday anyhow. What difference? It was sowed in the
Mammoths home colors, one word red and the next
word blue and the background white, same
shade as our stockings and letters and hats, and the
poem was by Grantland Rice. He died in the Summer of 54, July. Dutch and Joe and Clint and Egg
and Red went to the funeral, the brass. He was a
very fine man, the best. The poem was as follows.

FOR WHEN THE ONE GREAT SCORER COMES TO MARK
AGAINST YOUR NAME,
HE WRITES—NOT THAT YOU WON OR LOST—BUT HOW
YOU PLAYED THE GAME.

85

Thur June 21

Now that I think about it it must of been the following Thursday at that because I won Number 13 that day, 7-1 over Chicago, Chicago always a soft touch for me, and some of the boys drifted in, and they said, "Well, Author, getting past Number 13 is a sure sign you will achieve success," and I said I hoped so but rather not talk about it. "Do not leave your superstition run away with you," I said.

"13 is 13," they said. "Face the fact."

"Just forget the whole thing," I said. "Do not stand around putting the whammy on things."

"It is not an easy matter to forget," said the boys, and Red said the same, saying, "It is not an easy matter for the boys to forget, though I myself can put it out my mind in a minute."

"Mind over matter," said Piney.

"The Hall of Fame is not a thing to sneeze at," said Red, "for you are saying to the world, I am in the running for Fame so shove over the statue of the bust of Carl Hubbell a couple feet and make room for the statue of the bust of Henry Wiggen, and you will be sitting up in Cooperstown, N. Y., as long as the world spins. It is not the privilege of many men to live longer than their bones and their

86

flesh live. You must expect people to share with you in the struggle."

"I am not sneezing," I said. "I am doing exactly the opposite. It is all so true that it gives me the shakes. I do not ask you to forget it, then. Just fail to mention it. I do not wish to hear the name of Carl Hubbell."

"A good idea," the boys all said, and they never mentioned the name again, a good bunch of boys and no mistake. I said, "It is a beautiful poem."

"Anyhow it is a beautiful thought," said Red. "I am not too sure if it is a poem or not."

I knew I shouldn't of spoke on the subject of poetry with Red in the room.

"Could you write a better poem?" said Piney. "Who are you to say if it is a good poem or not? *You* never been a poet." He pounded it in the wall with nails.

"Was Carl Hubbell ever the President of the United States?" said Red.

"Not that I know of," said Piney.

"But who are you to judge or not," said Red, "if *you* never been the President?"

Piney backed off a way and looked at the poem. He takes Red serious, believing Red has a scientific mind. "I guess you are right at that," he said. "I guess you know. But it is a beautiful thought, then, even if maybe not a beautiful poem. Leave us leave it at that. One thing about it, it is mine." He give me a look.

It was, too. It come addressed in the mail to Piney, not me.

THIRD

THE SCHEDULE (continued)

30 NY at Bos; Sun July 1 NY at Brook (Doubleheader); Mon July 2 Open Date; Tues July 3 NY at Brook; Wed July 4 Wash at NY (Doubleheader, Independence Day, Ceremony); Thur July 5 Wash at NY; Fri

----

"The least you could do is wear a necktie," Piney said.

"Very well," I said, "go get one," and he took one off the hook. "Tie it on me," I said, "for if I tie it on myself you will only complain," and he tied it on, first on himself and then lifted it over his head and slipped it on mine and yanked it tight, and backed off a way and looked at me. "OK," he said. He straightened up the beds and pulled the window-shades even, and he took down the last couple naked girls still hung by friction. There was now nothing left in the way of drawings but the seamstitch, about 12 various poses, all dressed, or anyhow Piney's idea of the seamstitch beforehand, for she never did remember to send on a photo.

91

Tues July 3

He unstuck the motorcycle. "You know," he said, "if I could only someways blank out the girl on be-hind I could keep the motorcycle. I wish I could remember her name. Get off the bed, Author." He studied it awhile and breathed a deep breath and tore it up and threw it away, and he rung for the boy and told him go empty the basket, and the telephone rung, and he jumped—Piney I mean. "Stay calm," I said, "for I believe it is only Holly. I hope you do not mind me getting a fingerprint or 2 on the phone."

"That is OK," he said. He straightened the gui-tar on the hook, and he took down the letters, only the 2 letters all told plus a postal showing The Fed-eral Mart plus a raft more showing various views of The Geographical Center of the United States Motel, plus the wire which come just before we left for Brooklyn in the morning.

"Howdy," I said.

"Howdy," she said.

Then we said nothing for a minute.

"I am looking for the right thing to say," she said.

"Say what is on your mind," I said.

"The only thing on my mind is the name of that pitcher which I better not mention," she said, "for

I do not wish to run the risk of putting the whammy on things nor probably the double and triple hex besides."

Then we said nothing more for another minute. "Snap it up," said Piney. "She might arrive ahead of time."

"What did he say?" she said. "Did she arrive yet? What does she look like? I am interested in finding out if she is a looker."

"She ain't arrived," I said. "Nobody knows."

"Kiss me," she said. She kissed me a couple times in the phone.

"No," I said.

"Send him on an errand and kiss me," she said.

"He is expecting nothing in the mail," I said. "He is not interested in the paper. Are you having weather?"

"Terrible," she said.

"It is awful hot," I said.

"Plus tense," she said.

"Why tense?" said I. "It is only a baseball game. I won some and I lost some in my life. I won more than I lost. After all, I am libel to lose another ball game some day. You win and you lose."

"You ain't been losing much," she said.

"Just luck," I said.

93

"Plus skill," she said.

"Plus experience," said I.

"Plus good hitting by the boys, plus good field-ing," she said. "Michele been crawling in the yard all day without a stitch."

It is more than only luck," I said. "Luck plus arm."

"Certain records are meant to be broke," she said, "and others not."

"It been a record standing 20 years," I said. "Piney was the age of Michele when the record was set."

"Ask her the time," said Piney.

"What time is it?" I said.

"The clocks are all broke," she said. "Send him somewheres for the time," and I done so, and he went, and I kissed her a couple times in the phone until soon he come back. "It is 1930," he said, which in English means ½ past 7, and he set his watch and stuck the works in amongst his gear —the letters I mean, plus the postals and the wire. "Get a good sleep," she said. "Happy birthday. Rub your letters," and I said I would. I always rub up and down on my shirt a couple times before I face the enemy leadoff, rubbing the *W* and then the

E. It spells "we," meaning "us," and she knows I
am thinking of her, and we hung up.

"You must watch your swearing," said Piney,
"and I do not plan on finding your litter all over
the joint. Throw it out the window when you are
done."

"It ain't litter," I said. What it was, it was mes-
sages wishing me luck, hoping I would equal the
old record tomorrow and go on and bust it my next
time out. "Plus which I am not the kind of a citizen tosses his litter out the window." There was
also a wire from Carl Hubbell himself, "Good luck,
Author," and signed "Carl Hubbell," and I slipped
it out of the pile and clipped a hunk of paper to it
and wrote on the paper, "Save," and Holly saved it
for me, and also a wire @ me for the seamstitch
from the owner of the Motel, hoping she arrived
safe and telling me they was all pulling for me tomorrow back in The Geographical Center. I give
it to Piney to give to her, and I suppose he done so
sooner or later.

"Well," he said, "do not leave it laying around,
litter or whatever."

There come a bang on the door, and he jumped.
But it was only Dutch and Red, and Piney said,

"Please do not sit on the beds," and he went and dragged back 2 chairs from Horse and Ugly's room, and Dutch and Red sat down. It was unusual to see them together, for off the field they do not have too much use for each other. I can't remember they ever dropped in like that before, just the 2 of them.

"Do not take the mail too serious," said Dutch to me. "This time tomorrow night there might not be any word from anywhere."

"I been around," I said.

"I know you have," he said, and he thumbed through the stack a little, and then he pushed it away, and he whistled "From Maine To Georgia (July 4, 1776)" between his teeth.

"Like a march," said Piney, "not like a working song."

"1,000,000 pardons," said Dutch. He spit in the basket. Red got up and knocked his pipe out in the basket and loaded it again and flipped the match at the basket, and it missed, and Piney picked it up and opened the window and dropped it down and closed the window and pulled the shades even again. Dutch watched him and whistled. "Author," said Dutch, "I am about to bust a rule for the first time that I never busted before. I will give you your choice which game you rather work. Name your game."

"You are very kind," I said. "Either one is OK. Work me whichever game is best for the club."

"As far as I am personally concerned," said Dutch, "busting the record or not busting the record means no more to me than the situation in China. This been my policy all my life and always will. Choose your start, and after that I am the man in the driver seat again."

"Do not be a hero," said Red. "Pick the surest bet."

"Well," said I, "I naturally rather go against Littleman than Womack, for the boys are libel to hit Littleman fairly free."

"You vs. Littleman," said Dutch.

"Yes, that is best," said I. "Me vs. Littleman."

"Done," he said, and he crossed his leg the other way and looked at Piney, not speaking but only thinking, and after a long time he said, "As for you, I do not know what to tell you. You must be warned and cushioned for the shock of things. Red, give him the philosophy. Listen to Mr. Traphagen, boy."

97

Tues July 3

"It is almost 2000," said Piney. "I got to fly."

"Sit down and listen," said Dutch. "First things first."

"She will be landing," said Piney. "She will be landing."

"Which is exactly why you must soak up the philosophy," said Dutch, "while she is still in the air and sight unseen."

"I am in favor of the boy taking off," said Red. "I believe we can cover the matter still another time. There is time." Piney give him a look of thanks, and he looked at Dutch, and Dutch give him a look back, like you might give an insane individual. "Go," said Dutch, and Piney took off.

"Time?" said Dutch. "No, I say there is not time, no matter what you might think, Red. I am in the middle of the Summer and find myself not 3 games ahead—like we ought to been by now—but ½ as much, and I say there is not time. God help us. We got no catching on the bench. I will buy me a catcher over the Winter no matter what the cost nor no matter who I must swap in the deal. When I consider my catching I am the most miserable man on the face of the earth and wish that the day I was born was tore off the schedule at birth. That

98

boy is no good, I tell you, and I got no hope for him. He will never settle his mind on business. I need a catcher. I would give $800,000 cash plus any right-hand pitching Cincinnati might name plus any combination of 3 men except only Goldman, the Caruccis, Simpson and Roguski for Sam Mott of Cincinnati. I will even give George. He will be 31 in the Winter. I swear I would. I got no hope whatsoever." He got up and stretched and leaned against the door a minute. "Good luck, Author. Get a good sleep. Take a pill. I am going to take a pill myself, which I doubt will help in the slightest."

"There is plenty reason for hope," said Red, but Dutch already slammed the door behind. Red lit up his pipe again and flung the match at the basket again, and missed again. "So here is where my dictionary went," he said, "that I been looking all over for. Do you not believe in returning things?"

"Piney borrowed it," I said.

"Took it," said Red. "He never borrowed it. What is took or borrow to Piney? Give him the philosophy! What is philosophy to Piney Woods who is off to the moon on a motorcycle with a dream of a perfect and naked girl in his mind, and he will solve it all by science when he gets there.

Tues July 3

Do you know that he paid $22.50 for the reservation to the moon?"

"He paid $50," I said.

"Well, Dutch told me $22.50," said Red. "Maybe I did not hear him right. In my opinion it is $50 spent in the best possible way, for Piney has *got* to buy the moon, *got* to dream his perfect dream of science in outward space. You can not tell him otherwise. Give him the philosophy! He will either learn or he will not. I believe he will. He is a bright lad."

I took the basket in the bath. Then I changed my mind instead and walked Red down the hall and put the basket in Horse and Ugly's room. Theirs was all clean, and I swiped it, and Red knocked his pipe out in the sand can by the elevator. "Finally what Piney will find out is there is no place on earth like earth," said Red, "and he will find a woman less than perfect, and if he loves her all he can, and she loves him, and their children, too, that will be the nearest he can expect to the moon."

"What news from Rosemary?" I said.

"They will meet us in St. Louis," he said. "She got a postal your wife is pregnant again."

"So I know," I said, and the elevator come, and Red went on up, and I went back and laid down awhile in Horse and Ugly's room to keep from rumpling the bed. I might of slept. I don't know. It was just about dark when I went back, and I was sitting reading through the mail when they showed.

He kicked open the door, and his face was all tight and tense, and he stood there with her bag in one hand and the baseball Mike give her in the other, and he dropped the bag where he stood and lobbed the baseball on the bed, and he never said a word, only done a regular about-face like they learned him in the Marines, and that was the last I seen all night of Piney Woods. She watched him going off down the hall, so for a minute I seen only ½ her face, and then she walked in, and I give her my best TV smile. "Howdy," I said.

"You!" she said. "Ain't you ashamed? You!"

"In the bones," I said. "I tried 750 times being somebody else, but I guess we must end up making the best of bad bargains. What is up, Honey? Have a chair." She tossed her gear on the bed, and sat down, and then she popped back up and dug in her coat for her hanky, and then she sat down and waited for the cry, and soon it come, and she

101

cried for 5 minutes or more.

"After 3,382 miles by the map I land in the lap of the 2 snakiest characters in the country," she said. "Everywhere I went I run up against a snake here and there, but for every snake there was a dozen more. I am far from home. I wish I never left. They told me I never should of left. I should of listened. Do you not feel like 1½¢ worth of hamburger?"

"No doubt I am a snake," I said, "and a hamburger snake at that. Yet I believe I am in title to hear the charge against me."

"He never said a word from the time he took my bag," she said. "He looked me in the face and up and down, and he threw the bag in the cab, and he sat in his corner, and I in mine, and he looked out the window all the way."

"Here," I said. I give her a fresh hanky.

"No wonder you are roomies," she said. She looked all around. "Snakes with snakes. You stole my money and you never sent the acres but shoved it off on Piney, Snake Number 2, the both of you headed the quickest way for the Hall of Fame of Snakes."

"Did you eat?" I said.

"Not since supper," she said.

NY *at Brook*

"As far as the various charges go," said I, "I am no doubt guilty. Except I can now give you back your change," and I went in the bath and took the check out of the mirror, $6.85. "My punishment for all the rest is I sentence myself to buy you a dinner."

She thought this over, weighing how hungry she was against how angry. "I might as well," she said. She went in the bath and washed up. I rung for the boy and sent her bag up her room, and the baseball, and I took off the tie and hung it back on the hook. Then I changed my mind and put it back on again instead, probably not tying it in a very sensational way, however, and when she come out of the bath she looked better. She has nice skin. You might as well say that for her, and decent hair and eyes and nose, average, nothing below average and nothing too much above, just exactly the average kind of a girl you bump into everywhere you turn, waitresses and photo retouchers and switchboard girls, girls on trains and girls on planes, girls in depots and restaurants and nightclubs, girls in banks and insurance offices and tax offices, girls in the newspaper business and girls in the book business, girls selling tickets to the movies and girls tearing them in $\frac{1}{2}$ at the door, girls in

103

Tues July 3

Queen City and all the towns of the 4-State Mountain League, and girls in New York and Chicago, girls, girls, girls, everywhere I go. I guess I ought to know. I keep an eye peeled. There was nothing *wrong* with the girl for God sake. She may of been a tiny bit on the heavy side, maybe, but not so much that she couldn't strap it in shape once somebody showed her the ropes.

She grabbed her purse, leaving her coat behind, for the night was hot, and we took off. "Hi-ho, Silver," I said, "Away. To the Automat," and she smiled a little, the first time yet. It improved her 100% to see her smile.

"Author," said Abe, "I will be straining every muscle. I know you are going to win it." He kept sizing up the seamstitch in the mirror.

"I come 3,382 miles by the map," she said. "It is a sign. For when you add up the figures they come to 16, 3 plus 3 plus 8 plus 2."

"According to the radio there is a fellow confirms this on the electric brain," said Abe. "The brain calculates you will win it. It is the Hall of Fame for sure. The brain figures your lifetime record vs. Washington plus you being at your top in the probable hot weather plus Washington got mostly left-hand hitting plus the long fence plus the psychological advantages gives you the edge, Author." But he kept sizing her up in the mirror, and when I was paying the fare he leaned close to me and said, "Author, I am no back-seat driver, but I do not like the sight of you tramping around like this, you with one of the most charming and beautiful little women in baseball back home."

"But a trouble and a worry," I said, and I leaned closer still. "I know you will keep this confidential, Abe, but I am on solid grounds for divorce in 29 states. The charge is snakestitching, day and night, and sometimes even with the baby in her arm."

"What is this?" he said. "It is a joke."

"Ask anybody," I said, "only deep keep it confidential until it hits the court."

"I do not like it all the same," he said, "no matter what the reason. Best of luck tomorrow," and he drove off.

It was cool in there, and good, same old Automat. She ate about 35 nickels, nothing but sweets and starches, and she filled me in on her trip, things she left out of her letters. She begun to forget she thought I was a snake. By bus and train and cab and thumb she come, and finally by plane, the gift of the Motel man, and she took me back over every single one of the 3,382 miles word by word it seemed like. "But leave us talk about you," she said, and she asked me my most exciting experience, and I told her this and that, whatever come to mind, and I told her how I keep in shape in the Winter—light on sweets and starches, I said, heavy on the salads and lean meats until your weight was steady.

We drunk about 750 glasses of ice coffee, too much. She was mad about shoving nickels in the slot, and we watched the people come and go, sitting down with their food and folding open the paper, and every place you looked you seen the headline, WIGGEN FACES CRUCIAL TEST. I could not stop my heart from beating.

She loved watching the people, and she seen many a story, deciding who they were and what they done, and I told her she had the making of a private eye or a writer, and she said maybe, and we got a great laugh out of that. She said Piney said a girl could make a pile 750 ways in no time a-tall in a town the size of New York. "I hope so," I said, "though the thing about Piney is he is not experience in all the matters he believes he is."

"A snake," she said.

"No," said I, "lacking in experience and being a snake is 2 different things."

106

NY *at* Brook

She tucked it in the back of her mind for future filing. We did not talk too much about Piney.

And afterwards we walked uptown a couple blocks and looked in the windows, and soon we seen in a window this little statue called Really A Rhubarb, $2.98. It is run by water, a ballplayer and an umpire face to face, arguing, where first the ballplayer is leaning down shouting in the ump's face, and then the water shifts the balance and the ump is leaning down shouting in the ballplayer's face, back and forth, back and forth, back and forth, as long as the water lasts, I guess. You can buy a refill. No doubt you seen them for yourself, but she never did, and she laughed until she dropped, and I laughed along, too, though I seen such gadgets 750 times before.

She wrote down the store that sells them's address, and we rode the subway back home, the first time she ever rode one.

It was hot, and I could not sleep. I rung for the paper, and then I told the boy go borrow a couple Dozaway pills off Coker, and he brung them and said both Mr. Roguski and Mr. Smith said "Good night and good luck." The paper run a chart showing Carl Hubbell's consecutive streak game by game, 16, and alongside it my own, 15, and down below it said WILL THE AUTHOR DETHRONE KING CARL?, and up above they run these 2 pictures, Hubbell scowling and frowning at me, and me scowling and frowning back, very clever. I swallowed a Dozaway with water but it done no good a-tall. The necktie give me a headache was what it was, and the coffee was keeping me awake, plus which my heart was beating. I shouldn't of bought the paper.

Piney was not back. I kept expecting him any minute, for he seldom stays late on the town, but he didn't come. He wasn't back by morning neither. I laid there running up and down the Washington order, Lee and Scotch and Huff and Opper and Christensen and J. D. Williams. Once you get by J. D. you are in the clear, and I kept setting them down 1-2-3 in my mind, though then I drifted off and lost all control and woke up all in a sweat again and rung for warm milk, and I swallowed the other Dozaway, and then when I felt myself sinking the telephone rung, and it was this jackass—no need naming his name but you read his column—and he said, "Author, what is the story on your divorce? Who was that girl you was seen with?"

"Jackass," I said, and I hung up, and soon afterwards some kids begun blowing up fireworks in the street, and the cops come, only by the time they come the kids disappeared, and they sat there with their siren screaming, looking up and down the street. Finally I conked out. Maybe I slept 4 hours.

July 4 Wash at NY (Doubleheader, Inde-

We went to the park after breakfast straight from the Automat. The cabbie flew flags. The traffic was in a snarl already, early as it was. I was tired. In the clubhouse I borrowed a pair of dark glasses off somebody, and they made the sun easy on my eyes. I forget who. I also borrowed a stool and went up in the stands and sat beside her in the box. A cluck behind said, "Look at here, here is a bird with a stool," and his friend said, "A stool pigeon, you might say," and they laughed, and then they said it 14 more times and laughed 14 more times as well, and the seamstitch laughed the first 9.

She loved it, everything, all of it new and exciting and big to her, for she never seen it before except in pictures or on the TV, and it ain't the same thing. Most of all it was the color drove her hysterical, for she got a great eye for color. She looked better than she looked. A good sleep always done wonders for her, she said, or maybe she only looked better because once you hang with somebody awhile they look better, and everything she seen she admired.

"You would need all the threads of the rainbow to sow it," she said, the green and the brown of the field, and the white lines, and the blue of the sky, and the flags all waving on the roof, and the banners and bunting draped on the rails, and the band in their suits, for there was a band, it being the 4th, and their horns shone in the sun. When I was little, Pop told me the bands were in honor of my birthday on the 4th, and I believed him.

The boys begun strolling out and working up little pepper games, and she admired their suits, too, and the tan of their face, and the white ball bouncing soft on the green, and the sun now and then flashing off their bat, and the red of the outfield clay and the silver of the towers, and she admired the streaming of the people, all in their various colors, their hats and their shirts and their dresses, and the fans of the ladies. Somebody sent a straw hat spinning out of the upper deck, and it landed right side up near third base, and then it flipped over and Red come by and picked it up tried it on for size, and it did not fit, and the crowd howled, and he walked up behind George and tried it on George and it fell down over George's eyes, and the crowd howled still more, and Red tried scaling it back in the stands but it done the loop and fell back on the field near the enemy warm-up rubber. It laid there a long time. She got a great laugh out of that.

And the ushers in blue she even admired, and the peanut hawks in white, all moving and shouting every which way amongst the people. I bought her a card, a special souvenir deal printed for the 4th, and I showed her how to keep a book, who hit what and where. "Where do they flash the kind of a pitch that was threw?" she said.

"Where what?" I said.

"Where on the scoreboard?" she said.

"Scoreboards is for clucks," said I. "You decide by looking."

"Looking at what?"

"Looking at the *pitch*."

"I think I rather keep score like any ordinary cluck," she said. It was too hot to explain. It might not of been so hot if I wasn't so tired. The sun hurt my eyes, even through the glasses. The hawks carried no coffee. It was too hot. "I will take a Despadex," I said.

"You should of chose the first game while your energy lasts," she said. "Where is Piney?"

I was looking for him myself. But the boys was all up by now, all but Piney. "He ain't showed," I said. The scoreboard took his number down, 10, and stuck Jonah's in the slot instead, 18, and a little while afterwards they took out the whole bottom end of the order, Jonah and Coker and Van Gundy, 18, 7, 17, and stuck them back in different, 7, 17, 18, and she followed the matter, saying, "I guess Dutch does not consider Jonah Brooks much of a hitter."

"The only pitcher he bats in front of is me," I said.

"I guess Dutch must of give Piney the day," she said.

"I think Piney must of took it," I said. "What is give or took to Piney?"

"But does Dutch not consider such an act illegal?" she said.

"No more illegal than murder," I said.

It was S. R. O. only by now, 78 or 79,000, I forget. Behind us this cluck said, "A lot of people will not need to bother standing for the anthem nor the stretch, for they are standing already," and his friend laughed. Then they done this routine 14 more times.

Walt Womack come up out of the Washington dugout, the Wizard they call him, the Wizard of Washington. Yet nobody noticed him. They never do, not even down in Washington, not even the boys on his own club. He got no friends, no enemies. I myself talked to him 6 times at the most in my life, for he come to me in the matter of insurance. The boys on Washington all tell me he says 16 words per day most days, and 16 of these he cuts out on days he works. He sits in the lobby after breakfast smoking one cigar, and he pitches one baseball game and smokes one more cigar, and he eats dinner and smokes one cigar, and he goes to bed, no wife, no girl, loving 2 things and no other, loving to play baseball and loving money. Winters he referees football, and when football is done he referees basketball, keeping his legs strong, and his back, and his lungs. Maybe 6 times a Summer he spies me in the lobby, and he creeps up behind me and taps me on the shoulder and hands me a check for $1,000. "Here," he says, and I put it in his Fund, and he will retire from life at

114

47½ years with a check in the mail every month
to the age of 102. He tapped J. D. Williams
on the shoulder, and J. D. grabbed his mitt, and
they went down and warmed, and the sight of the
straw hat laying there annoyed him, and he picked
it up and folded it in ½ and leaned over the rail
and stuffed it in a trashcan. I watched him warm.
It is a pleasure to watch. He leans a long ways
forward when he throws, holding on to the ball
until the last instant, making use of every inch he
can stretch, throwing off the tips of his fingertips, a
hard fast-ball, a good curve, top control and a good
change-up, all in the same motion. You can not
read him. He got no habits you can spot. And he is
thinking, thinking, thinking, no thought in his
mind but the ball game, his ear and his eye nowheres but on the job, never a word, never a shout,
seldom a mistake, always backing up the right play
at the right place and always throwing to the right
base at the right time, a natural if ever a natural
lived, a good fielding pitcher and not a bad hitter
neither, fast on his feet, quick, strong legs, strong
back, and big lungs, a man of 30 that if you beat
him you know you wore your hitting clothes plus
horseshoes, for his stars never fail him more than 8
days a Summer. I consider him pretty near my

equal. She enjoyed watching Womack warm, too, and she got a great bang out of the drill in general, and the crew smoothing the infield, and the ceremony, and the anthem, everything. She even got a great bang when she seen the umps. "I hope there is a rhubarb," she said.

"It will be tight," I said. "A pitcher's game. Probably you will witness a rhubarb all right."

"I certainly hope so," she said.

Some tight. Washington went down 1-2-3, and so did we. Womack struck Sid Goldman out in the second. But Canada then followed with a single, our first hit, and Vincent Carucci with another, and they passed Coker to play for 2 on Van Gundy, a smart enough move only Van Gundy sent a little skittering ground ball down Bitsy Lee's way which Bitsy picked up and dropped, and picked up again and then threw wild, and 2 were in. Jonah slapped into the double play instead.

"I wonder why Piney Woods been benched," said the cluck behind.

"Pulled a muscle in Chicago," said Cluck Number 2.

"I did not notice," said the first cluck. "He was running OK in drill."

116

We picked up 2 more in the third, George and Perry singling, Pasquale fanning, but Sid laying a hold of one that went high and deep in right-center, and Harry Scotch begun giving chase, and I said to the seamstitch, "Never mind George, for George will score, but watch Perry on first," for Perry tagged up instead of roaming down the line, and Harry Scotch took it on the run over his shoulder, and Perry broke for second, and he beat the throw, sliding in under Bitsy Lee, and there was a rhubarb all right, Bitsy hopping up and down on one foot and then the other and telling the ump he put the tag on Perry, and the ump folding his arm and saying "No, no, 1,000 times no, young man," and the park all booing Bitsy and clapping for Perry, Perry himself scoring a minute later on Canada's single, his second of the day. He had a perfect day, Canada, 5 for 5, in the first game I mean.

"Now what they ought to do," said Cluck Number One, "is yank Van Gundy and slip Wiggen in and leave Wiggen get credit for the win."

"Probably he ain't warm," said Number 2.

"I do not think he would get legal credit anyhow," said Number 2.

"Who cares about legal? Change the goddam

law if it ain't legal. Give the man a chance to bust the goddam record."

"I wish you was," she said, "because I think the boys got on their hitting clothes."

"Womack will tighten," I said. "He ain't in real trouble. The first 2 runs was unearned."

"Tell me when he is in real trouble," she said.

Washington done nothing in the top of the fourth, and soon Womack was in trouble. George singled, and Perry done the same. He also had a good day, Perry, 5 for 4. In the first game. And Pasquale run out the count, and then he fouled a couple, and then he slammed one. It was gone. "0 plus 2 plus 2 plus 3 so far this inning equal 7," she said. "Author, you pulled a rock."

"Honey," I said, "I better go get dressed. Sit tight, for in a couple hours we will know the news. Then you wait here and do not move until somebody or other return," and I took the stool and started out.

"Where you going?" said Cluck Number One. "The legal ball game is 9 innings. Then in case you ain't up with the news there is another ball game following."

"Home," said I. "I forgot to blow up my fireworks."

It was slow progress, especially with the stool, for the aisles were overflowing. The score was 8-0 by the time I hit the clubhouse. Mick McKinney was sitting in front of the TV folding towels. "Howdy," he said.

"Howdy," I said. "Give me a Despadex."

He give me ½ a Despadex.

"This is for real," said I, "so give me the other ½."

"Sure," he said, though usually he won't. "It is false pep," he usually always says, but now he give me the other ½ and no argument, and I swallowed it down with cool coffee.

"Anybody seen Piney?" I said.

"He is in the tub," said Mick, which he was, sound asleep and snoring, his jacket for a pillow and his hat over his eye. "He showed in the middle of the lecture. Dutch fined him $200."

"Give me a rub," I said.

"Sure," he said.

"Was he drunk or something?"

"Nope. Just not too interested in baseball was all."

Coker hit a home run, Vincent aboard, 10-0. Blau was pitching for Washington by now. Coker later hit another home run. He had a good day in the first game. "I think I pulled a rock," I said. I laid down on Mick's table and shut my eyes. Between shutting my eyes and the Despadex I begun feeling better.

It was 12-1 in the seventh. Blau been replaced by Tiaffay for Washington, Tiaffay now replaced by Witt-Diamant, and Jonah Brooks drifted back in the clubhouse, told by Dutch to rest for the second game. Chocolate Barr took over the catching, the first big-league ball game he ever played in. He doubled in the eighth. Jonah loosened up his pants, and Mick brung him cool coffee, and he laid on the floor. "Hitting, man, hitting," said Jonah. "Do I hear a snoring?" He rose up and went over and looked at Piney all spraddled in the tub. "Peaceful, man," said Jonah, and he went and laid down again, and we talked about signs, and after awhile the boys got tired running the bases, and the ball game come to an end, 14-2, the first time we beat Womack since May, and me and Jonah drifted out. The crowd give me a terrific hand, and the band played "Happy Birthday," and I touched my hat and begun warming.

Soon Red come down and watched awhile and said if I was tired go tell Mick give me a Despadex, and I said I already done so, and he said if I wasn't afraid of a gamble go make him give me the other ½ as well. "Our pal Piney is in hot water," said Red.

"Or anyhow he is in the tub," I said, "catching up on the sleep I missed steering his girl around town. Think how nice to have a pal do your sleeping for you when you can not manage it yourself."

"Was she not the looker he hoped?" said Red. He walked around me, watching my motion. "Knock him down," he said.

"She is average," I said. He strolled down and stood by Jonah and told him a couple things, and Jonah listened with both ears, a smart boy, Jonah, knowing enough to listen to his betters, and a pleasure to pitch to, but no hitter. I threw him a couple fast-balls and they sunk just fine, and I was either warm or the Despadex took hold, and I didn't care which. We drifted back in.

Nobody spoke to me much. Somebody said "Happy birthday" and I said "Thank you kindly," and every now and again somebody passed me by and slapped me backhand on the tail, but nothing more. Everybody sat around drying off until Dutch and the brass come out from his office all smiles, and he stood on the scales and whipped out his glasses. Then he heard a snoring and whipped them off again and went and looked in the tub, and he put his glasses back on his nose and took the hat off Piney's face and seen Piney beneath, and he reached down and turned the water one full time around, and the boys all waited and watched, and soon Piney come slipping and sliding over the edge, and he looked up and down the line, his face all swole with sleep, and he doubled up his fist and said, "You stupid son of a bitches to try and drown a sleeping man."

"Be careful who you are calling stupid," said Dutch, and he laughed, and the boys all laughed along, seeing Dutch was. "It was I run the water, though not on a man but on a boy."

"Oh," said Piney. "Who won the ball game?" He sat down beside me, all dripping.

"Paris, France," said Dutch. "Guess the score."

"4-2," said Piney.

"Equal 6," said Dutch, "multiplied by the number on your back equal $60 fine for sleeping on duty, plus $200 from before equal $260. Holiday rates."

"What was the score?" said Piney to me.

"14-2," I said.

"OK," said Piney, "forget it then. I guess I can find out for myself."

122

Dutch went back up on the scale again, still all smiles. "Any new observations?" he said. "One nice way of putting the topping and icing on the holiday cake is bust their back again and spend the Summer coasting in."

"I believe Opper's arm is still bothering him," said Clint, meaning Sampson Opper of the Washington outfield.

"Then we will run on his arm," said Dutch. "May it fall off. As far as Littleman goes I expect we will encourage him back in the shower no quicker than is humanly possible. We never have trouble with him. Make him labor, for he will tire."

George spoke in Spanish to Red, and Red said "No," and Dutch said what did George say, never trusting Red all the way. "He says win this one for Author," said Red.

"No," said Dutch, "win this one for the column marked Win," and he lectured on what he said the night previous, no need repeating.

"Time," said Egg.

"Very good. Whitey Whiteside, stay ready," said Dutch. "Same order as before only Jonah bat 8 in front of Author. I hate to lose the power, yet I suppose a smart man behind the bat is better than a wet and sleepy boy. Good luck, Author."

July 4

"Good luck, Author," the boys all said, seeing that Dutch said it, and we straggled on out down the alley.

In the beginning things didn't go too good. The first pitch I threw I threw right down the pipe to Bitsy Lee, and he drilled it back over second. Yet we pitched him according to the book and would do the same again tomorrow, for if you read the enemy book you will see where we throw the first pitch of every ball game down the pipe to Bitsy Lee, and he always takes. Maybe 2 days all Summer he will cross us up, and today was the day, and he stood on first with one foot on the bag grinning at me, and I give him a grin back, a little colored chap no higher than your fist, very quick on his feet but still lacking science. "I pulled you a switch," he said.

"I got a great enjoyment watching you mess up that double play," I said.

"Hang on to the memory," said Bitsy.

Once on base he will look in for his sign, and then when he gets it he will start stunting up and down the line, and he done so, and me and Jonah knew the sign was flashed by now, the sacrifice. I threw to Sid, never so much to keep Bitsy close as to keep them from knowing we already had their sign, and then we threw twice to Harry Scotch, up under his chin, balls, both, good control. The whole park groaned, not knowing this was according to plan, and we watched Bitsy Lee out of the corner of our eye, and we seen the sign been switched by now, the hit and run. Most clubs believe you will not chance the pitch-out with the count 2 balls, and this is no doubt true of the ordinary pitcher, only I am personally far from ordinary. I rather waste a pitch, leave Jonah throw out Bitsy at second, and then go back and work on Harry Scotch, for even if I lose Harry he is nowheres so fast as Bitsy on the bases, and Jonah thought the same, and he signed for the pitch-out, and Perry picked up the sign, and I stretched and pitched, and I knew that behind me Perry was drifting to cover, and Bitsy Lee was steaming towards second, and I said to myself, or anyhow thought, "Bitsy, in another 5 seconds you will be dusting off your pants and jigging on back to your bench, and I will give you a grin again. I hope you got the philosophy to give me one back out of the same side of your mouth." And I also thought, "The whole park that just been groaning will change their tune in a hurry," and it all would of went according to plan only the pitch instead of floating wide to a right-hand hitter was in there, an inch too true, not more because Harry Scotch barely got wood on the ball, and he hit this puny little spinning type of a ground ball down through the hole left open by Perry.

I was now a little in the jam. "It is this false pep," said I to myself, "which sometimes makes you careless," and I went to work on Paul Huff, and the count went even at 2-2. He figured on the curve, so we poured the fast-ball through instead, and what he done he swung late and topped it, and it dribbled down the line, and I raced over, faking Bitsy Lee back into third, and Jonah come down the line crying, "Play it, man, play it!" and George cried from third, "Huégelo! Huégelo! Huégelo!" which in Spanish means "Play it!" 3 times, for I played Winter ball both in Mexico and Cuba, only I figured they was both wrong, I was on top of it, and I seen it would roll foul, and I hung over it, ready to pounce and collar it the instant it crossed the line, only then it never done so, and all hands was safe, the enemy on every base, and I was in the jam for real. "False pep," said I to myself, "plus sitting in the Automat when I should of been asleep, plus standing in the night air laughing at Really A Rhubarb, plus jackasses on the telephone and these juvenile minds blowing up fireworks plus the stupid police. May they all rot in Hell, and may flood and fire and 750 plagues of snakes strike Good Hope, Georgia, the home of Piney Woods."

We held a conference, and we all agreed never mind the run, play for 2. The boys all went back to their spot, and I pitched low and outside to Sampson Opper, and careful, and we run the string out. That suited me fine, too, for he seen my control was good. He would never dare give the curve the go-by. Yet he would never get the fast-ball neither, not from me. The park was absolutely quiet. You heard nothing but the peanut hawks until they also stopped to see the pitch, and I toed in, and then somebody in the band give a little toot on his goddam horn, and I toed out again, and Washington picked it up, and their bench begun screaming, "Toot! Toot Toot! Toot Toot Toot!"

It was a perfect pitch I finally threw, hooking out and away from a left-hand hitter, and he lifted it up in short left, a soft fly ball that George or Coker might of took over their shoulder if they been lay-ing normal. But they were playing for 2. I figured Vincent Carucci would gather it in, and I hustled to third to cover for George. Coker was hollering "Vincent! Vincent!" but Vincent was too deep and he hollered back, "No! George!" but George seen it was not for him. "Tómelo! Tómelo! Yousted! Vincent! Tómelo!" ("You grab it, Vincent, for it is beyond my reach!") and they broke their step, both of them, Coker alone still giving chase at top speed, and getting his glove on it and falling. I remember he raised the white of the line, a little cloud, and Vincent Carucci went sailing over, his legs tucked up under him so his spikes would stay free and clear, and George went after it, chasing it in foul territory near the rail. Harry Scotch went by towards home, and Paul Huff, too, round and round like in a bad dream, and then he come up with the ball—George I mean—and also with a length of banners and bunting hanging off the rail, and at last he undone himself and found the handle and whipped it back, and I put the tag on Opper sliding in.

The park begun booing all of a sudden, "Boo-oo-oo-oo-o," for they seen Dutch standing in the dugout. But Dutch ain't lifted me in the first inning since the night of Friday, April 24, 1953, the coldest April 24 in history everybody said. He strolled down the line and took a drink from the bubbler and went and sat back down again.

And I got hot then, setting down 7 men in a row, Christensen and J. D. Williams, and then the bottom end of the Washington order in the second, and I fanned Bitsy Lee in the top of the third, and I fooled Harry Scotch on a change-up that he bounced right back to me. He begun jigging on down towards first, no chance in the world, and I held the ball a second, not throwing, and he turned his head and looked at me, wondering, and he seen I still was holding it, and he begun running serious now, and finally I threw to Sid and nipped him by a step, and on his way back to the dugout he shouted at me, "Author, you stink. It is a hot day for running."

"I do not want you developing lazy habits," I said. I was feeling pretty good all of a sudden, all full of the old confidence, or maybe only Despadex, throwing as hard and as fast now as I ever threw a baseball in my life, and I threw 2 extremely fast-balls to Paul Huff, and he never seen them, only swung, and they sunk, breaking down and under, and then I threw another, but it never sunk, never broke, and he swung again. I heard it go by. I never seen it. One base.

July 4

Jonah looked in at the bench, and Dutch told Red jiggle the phone, and Red done so, and Whitey Whiteside begun warming. Behind the fence along the bullpen the clucks all booed Whitey. "Down! Down!" they shouted, and somebody tossed a fireworks in the bullpen, and soon there was more, popping and cracking and dying and smoking, Whitey and Chocolate Barr running out on the field crying "Time," while behind them the fireworks come down in a regular storm and blaze, and the umps called "Time" and sent a couple cops to the bullpen, and a couple men from the crew come with a hose and soaked the fireworks. Whitey and Chocolate Barr went back and warmed, the cops standing by, their arm folded looking up in the crowd.

It might not of meant a thing, the bad pitch. It was hard telling. It was the first bad pitch I threw all day. Yet I suppose I knew I was dead, no sleep to write home about, the false pep no good for long without genuine pep to start with. Jonah signed, "Try another," and we tried another, low to Sampson Opper where it would do the least damage, and it did not sink, and Opper whaled it, a low hard drive that Sid dove for and got his hand on but could not hold, too hot to handle,

Huff and Opper both safe, and Jonah come down the line, and Dutch come out, and the boys all gathered round. The fans booed Dutch, loud and long until your ears begun itching.

"What do you think?" he said.

"2 in a row had nothing," said Jonah. "No sink, man."

"I might try another try," I said.

"It is a right-hand hitter," said Dutch, meaning Christensen of Washington, a right-hand hitter.

"I wish it was otherwise," I said.

"Risky try, man," said Jonah.

"Deep down," said Dutch, "tell me deep down in the cellar of your heart what you think. I will leave it to you."

"I ain't with it," I said.

"Very good," he said, and he give the wigwag for Whitey, and Whitey come strolling in, the clucks booing Whitey and Dutch both by now. "The boys will save it for you," said Dutch, "and you will cop Number 16 your next rotation." It was my game to lose now, but not win. The best I could hope for was no decision.

I give Whitey the ball. "I will save it for you," he said, and I walked off. The booing changed to clapping all of a sudden in a second, and I touched my

131

July 4

hat. In the dugout the boys all said, "We will save it for you, Author," but I said nothing, only give Piney a look. He was sitting in the corner whistling a tune, his cheeks puffing out and in, staring straight ahead, never at me, looking fresh like you look when you just enjoyed the most delicious snooze, 100%.

Mick was in the clubhouse, nobody else. He was pouring little bottles of liniment in big ones. He said nothing. I said only one word to him. It is spelled with 4 letters. No need repeating. Later I told him turn off the stupid TV. But that was all.

I sat in the shower, and then I put on my clothes. Mick was sitting on a stool in the corner with the radio glued against his ear. "Score," I said.

"3-1," he said. "We are making it back. Top of the fifth. Whitey been holding them off fine. So is this Littleman, however."

"I only asked the news," I said. "Never mind the editorials."

"Buck up," said Mick. "The game ain't over until the last man is out."

"Turn loose your stool," I said, and he got up off his stool, and I took it, and I put the dark glasses back on and went out the door and down under the stands. Up above it was like the roar of thunder,

132

now the roar, now the silence, now the pitch and then the roar again. It was cool down there. I went around and up the third-base side to the box again.

"Look at here," said Cluck Number One. "Where was you, stool pigeon? You missed history."

"I was looking from a closer angle," I said.

"What closer angle?" said Number 2. "What is closer than $3.15 seats?"

"They will save it for you yet," she said. "Have a peanut."

"Peanuts fat you up," I said.

"Is that right?" she said. She folded the top of the bag down tight and set them on the ledge. "Who runs the scoreboard?" she said.

"Just watch the ball game," I said. "You paid $3.15 for the privilege."

Sid Goldman hit a homer in the bottom of the sixth, a long, low drive that cleared the wall where the stands meet the bleachers, and Canada Smith almost put them back to back, and the park screamed, only then the drive sunk, and Harry Scotch was waiting, and the screaming sunk with it into silence.

Littleman struck us out in the seventh, Vincent, then Coker, then Lawyer Longabucco, Lawyer hitting for Jonah. "He got the face of a thief and a moron," she said, meaning Littleman.

"No," said I, "he is a fine and pleasant country boy throwing for groceries, a second-rate pitcher on a first-rate day. That happens, too."

"I got a lot to learn," she said.

"You will learn."

Chocolate Barr done our catching in the eighth, and Whitey set Washington down again, still strong. Dutch lifted him for a hitter in our ½, Willis Tyler, but we done nothing, and Horse done our pitching in the ninth. "Supposing you ever run out of pitchers?" she said. "Who would pitch?"

"3-Finger Brown," I said.

"3-Finger Brown died some years back," said Cluck Number One, and him and Number 2 begun arguing the date when 3-Finger Brown died.

"You are a great kidder," she said, and she give me a wink. She was quite attractive winking.

Then all in a moment everything changed. That's how it happens. You are sitting feeling sorry for yourself, and then the break comes, and where a minute ago it was the afternoon of the 4th of July all of a sudden there is no afternoon a-tall, nothing, only the sweating of your hand, and the sweat running down under your arm, and your heart starts beating. Pasquale popped out to open our ninth, but Sid singled, and Wash Washburn pinch-run for Sid, and a good move, too, for Canada singled and Wash went to third and never stopped but faked the dash for home and drew the throw off Harry Scotch, a fine heave, clear to the plate from medium right, the only play Harry could of possibly made, and Wash hurried back to third and Canada took second and the park went mad.

She was up and screaming now. The whole park was on their feet. I could see nothing. What was to see? They would pass Vincent and play for 2, which they done. "What is Piney doing?" she said.

"Where?" I said, and I stood up. "He is choosing a bat."

"What is the other boy doing?" she said.

"That is no boy," I said. "That is Ugly Jones."

"What is he doing?"

"He is also choosing a bat."

"What is Coker Roguski doing?" she said. "Is he in a rhubarb with the ump?"

"He is gassing with the catcher. It is his habit."

"Is he not in a nervous sweat?" she said.

"He is thinking while gassing," I said. "When you are hitting you are thinking. You got too much to concentrate on besides sweating."

135

July 4

"I would be," she said.

"You did not play 77 games already approximately," I said, "nor plan on playing 77 more before the Summer is out."

Then the whole park groaned, for Coker popped up, and Piney and Ugly stood on the dugout step, and then Ugly sat back down, and Piney advanced forward swinging 3 bats. "Why all them bats?" she said.

"To make his own feel lighter," I said.

"Why not choose a lighter bat to start with?" she said.

"It is the custom," I said.

"I can not hear you," she said. She was leaping up and down. I believe she must of took off a pound and ½ at least while Piney was at the bat, leaping up and down, and the whole park besides. I never heard such a noise in my life before nor since. He fouled a couple off. Then he fouled another, and Paul Huff raced over from third and stood by the rail waiting, reaching and waiting, reaching, reaching, but it fell in, maybe 4 rows back, and the park let out their breath again, and the next pitch Piney whacked solid and drove it down the middle, a wicked smash, a sweep hitter

136

they call him, and Littleman ducked down but
stuck up his hand, both at the same time, wishing
to save his skin and yet also collar the drive. It
was like it was shot out of a cannon, all the power
behind it of a young man not yet 21 who could be,
without hardly straining, a motorcycle racer and a
guitar player and an explorer in outward space all
at once, and it glanced off Littleman's glove and
popped high in the air near second base, and Bitsy
Lee was standing waiting when it come down, and
he left it settle in his glove, and then he picked it
out with his meat hand and stuck it in his pocket,
a souvenir of the day my streak was broke, and he
jigged off to the visiting clubhouse, and the whole
park groaned and was silent, and they sat down.
"What in the world happened?" she said.

"The game ended," I said.

Then they stood up, and they filed out. On the
top of the roof I seen the crew lowering the flags.
They were fairly quiet—the fans I mean—1,000's
and 1,000's and 1,000's of clucks, out the exits, out
across the field, stopping by home plate and sizing
up the fences like they do, and stopping by the hill
and looking down towards home. And the fences

look far, while home plate looks close from the hill. They think the pitcher got the best of things, Maybe so. But the fences are closer than they look, and the spaces behind you are wide, and the batter got wood in his hand, and maybe you are strong, for you got to be strong to pitch, but the batter is also strong, and the ball is lively, and you got a brain, yes, but the batter also got a brain, and you guess him, and he guesses you, and one of you has got to lose the decision on every guess. If the both of you are lucky you guess right enough times, and you keep your job, which is what it also is, your job I mean, your rent and your baby-food. The crew begun covering the infield. "What is the sense in covering it?" she said. "They only got to uncover it tomorrow."

"Honey," I said, "you wait here again and do not move until somebody or other return," and I took the stool and went back across the field and in the clubhouse.

Everybody was all full of 750 apologies and regrets, and the writers all asked me how I felt, and I said, "Lousy. How else?"

"Say something," said the writers. "Give us a good Henry Wiggen-type statement."

"No comment," I said. "You can not win them all."

And the writers cleared out and the boys all showered and sat around drying. Everybody in a good mood. It was the 4th of July and 1½ games on top, the Summer ½ done, and I sat amongst them, and everybody was very kind and polite like you are when somebody suffered a blow, and I said to the boys, "Boys," said I, "I will bet nobody can guess where Piney's guitar went."

They all guessed, guessing these foul and crazy places, no need repeating. "No," I said, "it is hid on the 13th floor."

"There ain't no 13," he said.

"It is the floor above 12," I said, "no matter what they call it, which if you do not take the seamstitch off my hand I will drop the guitar out the window from the floor above 12 to the street below."

"She ain't much of a looker," he said.

"She come 3,382 miles by the map," I said. "She is a better looker today than she was yesterday and will improve with time with polish and seasoning. She is still greener than spinach. So was we all not long ago."

"I will sue you," he said. "I got witnesses."

July 4

"To what?"

"To you said you threatened to dropping the guitar out the window."

"Who? I said such a thing as that? Me? Who heard me?" I placed my hand on my chest.

"I never heard him say any such a thing," said Horse.

"Nor I," said Ugly.

Up and down the line the boys all shook their head. "We never heard him say any such a thing," they said.

"Nor we doubt he could be capable of any such a foul and dirty deed," said Red. He put it all in Spanish for George, and George was laughing.

"There is such a thing as a lie detector," said Piney.

"You got no witnesses," I said, "for you got no friends. You got only dreams. I suppose you *got* to have dreams. Still and all, dreaming will not patch together again a guitar smashed in pieces from 13 stories up."

"Maybe she will soon leave town," he said.

"She only got a check for $6.85 to her name," I said. "She is libel to be around almost forever."

"I was fined $260," he said. "I am broke."

"You will need only Automat nickels. Here. She

140

is waiting in the box," I said. I had 8 or 10 nickels left over from breakfast and I give them to Piney. "Hand me your hat," I said, and he took his hat off the hook, and I went up and down the line, and the boys all dug in their pants and threw nickels in the hat. I don't know how much, but it was some, enough, and he dumped them in his pocket and hung his hat back on the hook, and he left by the alley, and I did not see him again until very late.

When he come home he had this gadget with him, Really A Rhubarb, and he set it on the dresser and started it in motion. "Watch," he said, and I watched, but nothing happened. "I was robbed," he said. He picked it up and shook it and set it down again, and nothing happened again. "$2.98 down the hatch," he said. "A swindle. I will never again trust anybody with a 10-foot pole."

"Most people you can trust," I said. "Some not."

"Yourself I suppose?" said Piney. "Author, I been reviewing matters in my mind, and I been struck with a thought. Do you remember the $10 bill she sowed to the letter? Do you remember what become of it? You stuck it in your pocket."

"I give her the change back last night," I said.

141

July 4

"So I seen," he said, "for I seen the check. But the check was $6.85."

"The ticket was $3.15," said I, "plus $6.85 equal $10."

"But it was I that bought the ticket, yours truly Piney Woods. $3.15 of the $10 stuck to you."

"I guess it did at that," I said.

"It is no wonder you are rich," he said. He shook Really A Rhubarb one more time and set it down again and give it a look.

"Why not try the science of filling it with water?" I said.

He went and filled it with water and come back and set it on the dresser again, and it worked, and he laid on his bed looking up at the drawings of the seamstitch. He reached up with his toe and nudged them off, and they drifted down on the floor.

"Did you have a decent time?" I said.

"Pretty good," he said, "though the thrill is gone from shoving nickels in the Automat."

"The island is full of restaurants," I said.

"No doubt you realize restaurants cost money, which $260 in fines is libel to leave me short to payday."

"Dutch will kick it back when you begin concentrating," I said.

142

"In the meantime I am short. Maybe you could loan me a couple dollars, Author."

"Meaning what?" I said.

"About 50?"

"How about 25?" I said.

"Done," he said, and I sat up and reached in my wallet and passed across the $25, plus also $3.15, $28.15, and I laid back down again, and he sat up and shoved it in his pocket and also laid back down again, and we laid there watching this gadget, Really A Rhubarb, the ump first leaning down shouting in the ballplayer's face, and then the water shifted the balance, and the ballplayer now leaned down shouting in the ump's face, and we laid on the beds watching and laughing, the first time in my life he ever laughed so hard, and it went back and forth, back and forth, as long as the water lasts, I guess.